The Last Oracle
& Other Ghostly Tales

Jennifer Rachel Baumer

Monstrosity Ink

Reno, Nevada

The Last Oracle
& Other Ghostly Tales

Copyright © 2013 by Monstrosity Ink
Published by Monstrosity Ink

Cover art © copyright 2013 by Jennifer Rachel Baumer

Book and cover design copyright (2) 2013 by Monstrosity Ink

ISBN – 13: 978-0615904061 (Monstrosity Ink)
ISBN – 10: 0615904068

"*(How to Tell) The Danser from the Danse*" © 2013
Originally appeared in Dark Recesses, Cutting Block Press, July 2010
"*The Little Cat in the Attic Window, The Blue House on the Corner*" © 2013
Originally appeared in Challenging Destiny #24, August 2007
"*The Return*" © 2013
"*The Book of Halves*" © 2013
"*Housewarming*" © 2013
"*In the Shape of a Heart*" © 2013
This story originally appeared in Quantum Muse, 2004
"*Early's Garage: We'll Fix It*" © 2013
This story originally appeared in Liquid Imagination 12, 2012
"*On the Squad*" © 2013
"*The Last Oracle*" © 2013
Originally appeared in Clarity, February 2005

Monstrosity Ink

Table of Contents

I've always loved the Danse Macabre at Renaissance Fairs, the swirling dance, the bone rattle of drums, the skeletal masks. Originally the dancers were meant to remind viewers that death can strike at any time – but today death passed them by.
And then I started to wonder: what if the dancers <u>didn't</u> pass by?

(How to Tell) The Danser from the Dance

Because I could not stop for Death
He kindly stopped for me
~ Emily Dickinson

The day sounds like silver. Wind chimes dangle from trees to light the way up the canyon. The heady smell of eucalyptus and Timothy grass rises in the heat. A haze of clouds covers the Marin sky. Morris dancers moving out of shade and shadow flicker into existence and out.

Robert holds Gwen's hand tightly, weaving between colorful tents, handmade gowns thrown over tree branches, ceramic goddesses perched on temporary hearths, leather masks on display. Silver catches sunlight at jewelers and foundries, shines off peace-tied weapons and silver flutes. The bright air sounds with falcon cry, answered by an errant hawk watching his park consumed for the long weekend.

It's midday, the lords and ladies growing thick in the canyon and hot beneath their Elizabethan finery; soon the faire will smell authentic. Gwen lets him pull her through the crowd, her fingers tight on his. He nearly lost her last week—or the week before; it was Saturday then and it's Sunday now, does that make it week before last? When the semi had lost control on the bridge and the sounds had been screaming and tortured metal and flesh and the smell of fear and some broken thing from the truck or her car and the smell of the highway patrolman's cologne that finally made her vomit over and over on the asphalt, the transport driver *still* motionless behind the wheel of the truck.

"Stop it," Robert says.

It's not like she hasn't tried. But it sneaks up on her at the least likely moments. Or maybe they are likely—times when she's truly happy she can't help but think how close she came to never having those moments again.

"Will you stop?" He laughs and pulls her into his arms. A bawdy voice behind them exclaims, "My good sir! To treat a lady such in public—"

"But surely she has already lost much of her clothing," a woman's atrocious English accent puts in. "My girl, come to my shop. I can replace the garments this ne'er-do-well has clearly torn from thee!"

Gwen giggles. "M'lady, I would be so bold—I like the way I dress!" She's wearing cut offs, long enough to hide the bruises from the steering wheel, and a tank top because the bruising of her breast bone is all internal. The cuts and bruises otherwise are healing. It's summer, and she's all but in the pink. Or in the green.

They leave the merchants behind, wander toward the food court because there are meat pies and turkey legs and chocolate covered raspberry clusters and because they haven't decided what to buy and because jousting knights are taking a break. The Queen passes them on the way and they fall back from the path among the trees, bowing and curtseying low as the jester slips past and the bells chime, and she hears voices raised, women's voices, as if they're caroling the generous Queen.

"The Queen doesn't appear to be padded," Gwen says, still bowing. She sees her disreputable Nikes, the leaf-littered dirt that smells strong at midday, the—

"Robert?"

His hand is no longer in hers. Her fingers spasm, grabbing for him. She yanks her head around, whiplashed muscles protesting, but he's not behind her, and she panics. This isn't like him, Robert doesn't just go off and leave—even if they were apart during the faire they'd have made arrangements to find each other again, and when, and where. "Robert!"

Everything hurts—arms, legs, back, hips—but she spins as fast as she can. The clearing is almost empty. Everyone else has stepped back onto the path in the wake of the Queen.

"*Robert!*"

One of the women on the path reaches toward her. "How old—?"

"My husband," Gwen says and the woman looks perplexed and moves on.

"What's wrong?"

His fingers tighten on hers. Gwen almost screams and jolts up out of the curtsey and Robert is beside her and her heart is pounding almost as hard as it did that day last week—or week before last—when there was the sound of scorched metal and the trucker sat so still behind the wheel—

"We can go any time you like," he says. He's moved to stand directly in front of her, his hands holding hers. She can look right at him, focus only on him, and everything else will go away. "I thought it might be too soon—

Gwen lets out a long, long breath, relaxing back into her body. "It's all right. I just—lost track for a minute. I'm all right. I don't want to go." She takes a look around and points. "Look, there's the leather workers you wanted to see. Let me buy you a wallet."

She tugs him this time. A dog with a silver tankard around his neck runs between them, a trio of small children in mostly homemade dress streak in front of Gwen, so close she goes up on tiptoe to avoid running into them. From around them she hears "G'day" and "G'morrow" and "M'lady, m'lord," and the one crazy woman, her hair a shambles of spider webs and dried leaves, "Buy my lovely carrots, sirrah? Buy my lovely posies? Ach, what a lovely pair of dumplings, sir—" and Robert gives a squeak. Gwen guesses the carrot woman has grabbed his ass, so she must not be that crazy after all, but Gwen doesn't stop or look back, she just runs, laughing, the teal and white striped leather worker's tent in front of them. Masks hang from trees, ornate and fanciful, beautiful and expensive, like woodland sprites and moons and stars, faeries and animals, the masks worked elegantly with diamond eyeholes and cats' eyes and leaf eyes. Before they reach it she hears the flutes and tambourines again, and a hollow drum this time. She goes completely still, a thrill of fear rising through her and Robert moves ahead, pulling at her hand.

"Is that the Queen again? Doesn't she ever stay put?" When she doesn't answer, he turns back. "What?"

"It's not the Queen," she says.

Bone flute. The shrill sound makes her own bones ache. The empty drum is the sound of a dead heart beating. The clear morning air carries the sound clearly. Long before they're in sight she knows what's coming.

Skeletal dancers. Hooded players. They caper and grin, rictus mouths and blank black eyes, clawed hands at their music. They move like the jester did, knees high, gestures exaggerated.

"Morris dancers," Robert says, and then, "No, I mean danse macabre." His hands tighten on hers. "They played to remind people that—" He falters. She can already figure out what they represent, the bone white and death black amongst the sun-warmed green glen.

"That death was passing you by and you should enjoy life." He squeezes her hands again, as if to pull her away.

That isn't quite it, she thinks. It was that death *had* passed you by but that you could never anticipate what would happen tomorrow. "Eat drink and be merry," she says. "For tomorrow—"

But at the look in his eyes, she doesn't finish. The dancers have almost disappeared into the glen, the wailing music fades and her heart stops pounding hard enough to break through her chest wall. Two more urchins run between them, breaking the clasp of their hands. Gwen calls over them. "Do you want—" she starts, and sees his face change, an expression of terror, eyes wide and horrified, mouth open. He reaches for her, grabs and misses. He says her name, she can see his mouth move but she can't hear him because the music screeches so loud, so high, Gwen presses her hands over her ears and squeezes her eyes closed, sound a physical, hurting presence. "Please," she says. One hand comes away from her ears and reaches for Robert.

A hand takes hers. Thin, brittle fingers wrap around her hand. She is pulled into motion, the music filling her like her pulse, beating through her. Her blood sings with the bone flute. Her heart pounds to the hollow drum. The tambourines drive her, eyes dazzled when she opens them to a silver world, the dark figures capering through it nothing more than shadows on a screen of liquid silver, rippling through with music, shot through with points of light. Her mouth is full of the bitter taste of ashes and she cannot speak. Past the fear, something observes, catalogs what's happening.

They pull her forward. There are four of them, rail thin skeletons cavorting, black hooded seers spinning and gliding. She can't tell who holds her hands and she feels her feet pick up the rhythm. She is no longer being led; she has taken up the dance.

There is no tunnel, no beckoning light. No clichés, no obvious trappings. The fear rises in her until she chokes on it but she follows, dancing, calling with no voice.

In the glen, just beyond the teal and white leather worker's tent, Robert's hands close convulsively on empty air. "Gwen? *Gwen!*"

A woman passing on the path between shops stops and reaches

toward him. "How old—?"

"My wife," he says.

She gives him a peculiar glance and moves on.

There's a Lost & Found tent. In it are a variety of children eating ice cream. The attendants here pay only cursory attention to medieval dress. They talk like normal human beings. It's something of a relief.

Or it would be. If she were here.

No point asking—"have you seen?" Gwen is an adult. If lost, she'd make her own arrangements to be found. If lost, she'd say so.

Besides, she is not among the ice cream eaters.

"Gwen," he says aloud. His voice is wistful. The wistfulness scares him.

"How old is she?" The girl wears an official yellow T-shirt and a pseudo Edwardian vest over it. Her bright yellow hair is in braids.

"My wife," Robert says, distracted.

"Try the gate," the girl tells him. "Lots of couples meet there."

Like a dating service, he thinks, confused. He blunders into the tent flap and has a moment's claustrophobic panic before he's free. A small child just outside the entrance looks up at him with lost eyes and says, "Daddy?"

"No," Robert says. Shouldn't *she know?*

Gwen is not at the gate. Ribbons dance in the wind there. Flags snap over the tents where wenches take Master Card and Lord Visa and tie plastic bands around celebrants' wrists. Someone gives him a lemon yellow hand stamp before he leaves the event. Robert runs, white legs flashing under shorts. One of the shuttles passes him in a noxious roaring cloud of natural gas fumes. They parked almost a mile away.

And why would she have gone back to the car without you?

Because she panicked. She's not all right yet. It's only a week since the accident. Cut her some slack.

He runs.

In the silver world, she sees the bridge again. It beckons, just past the canyon where the Ren Faire is. And that's wrong, Gwen thinks, but she doesn't have time to worry about it. The shadow dansers pull her along quickly and the music takes up residence in her head. Her thoughts idle. Her feet move. She knows this dance, as if it's part of her, and the fair-goers part before them, letting the Danse Macabre through.

There, in front of them, a young mother and her baby, the child decked out in sunflowers and leaves, the mother beaming, grinning. Gwen winces as they pass. The woman was diagnosed with breast cancer, barely beat it. Every day she checks, obsessive, a morning ritual driving her apart from her husband but she can't stop.

Death passed you by, Gwen thinks. One of the seers prances close to the young woman and her smile dips, becomes uncertain. She holds the child closer and it cries, discomforted, but the seer moves on, blind eyes hidden under the hood of the robe, eldritch fingers clearing a path through the fog they dance through.

One of the other seers moves beside her, all thin arms and brittle fingers, takes her hand. A thrill of nausea wracks her but her body is light, strong. Gwen dances, dances, watches the people along the paths fall back, some laughing, others repulsed. None of them are Robert. She needs to find him soon. Before he starts to worry. She's clung so close this last week.

The dance moves forward. A young man in leathers in front of them doesn't turn or move, doesn't seem even to hear them. Gwen squints, the bone flute so loud it hurts, the drum so hard it beats inside her: she couldn't not dance if she tried. They wail and spin, closer now, and he only turns at the last minute. The flautist is first there, legs high, fingers arched atop the keys of his silver flute, he passes *through* the man whose expression changes from dullness to terror in an instant.

Gwen balks, pulling back against the seer's bony hand. She flails and shouts, desperate that someone along the path might see she needs help and pull her free.

The seer hisses and throws her forward brutally. Gwen trips and falls, her hands out in front of her, so they slide through the man, Gwen stumbling free of him with a snap and tug, as if she pulled herself free of mud. The man behind her now. The man on the ground, bloody hands scrabbling at blood caked asphalt, helmet rolled free, hands broken, legs, back. Head injuries. Internal injuries. Asphalt and the sound of the traffic that hasn't stopped yet, almost comforting compared to the blaring radio and the concerned looks of drivers, the still form behind the steering wheel, the—the—motorcycle, wheels bent, too many injuries, we couldn't— He shouts something suddenly and Gwen snaps back into herself. Into the dance. They are all around her, shadow shapes, shadow dansers. The dance feels so good, to move, to live, but she has to get free, get away, get back to Robert—

***

"Come on, Gwen, pick up. Pick up." She had her phone, he'd made certain she brought it. He was the one without today, the one off in the parking lot at a payphone, calling, searching the whole time. Had she turned it off or set it to vibrate? But she had it in her pocket, he remembered she had peered in the mirror at it and said something about it looking like a pack of smokes. It was set to vibrate because she couldn't turn it off anymore, something had happened to it in the accident and the battery shorted— when she turned it off she had to remove and replace the battery to make it work again.

Gwen's phone rang a sixth time without voice mail picking up and that was when he knew something was really wrong.

Knew it, or finally admitted it.

The seer wouldn't let go of her hand. Twilight had begun to filter into the glade. September days, at equinox, were short. The year was turning. *Dying*. She panicked again at the word and pulled again at the seer, pulled free but the music buoyed her up, the steps carried her forward, the flautist behind her now, prancing with endless energy, driving her. They swirled, bone-white masks, rictus grins, black dresses and robes flying from them and Gwen caught up again, dancing. She watched the people along the path, searching for Robert, danced and spun and people stepped back from the Danse Macabre, small children pulled aside by mothers, couples held hands and ran before them, laughing. Until the old man, white hair, blue eyes.

His wife had turned aside to look at sheet music beside the harpist's tent, and he stood, relaxing in the late day sun, unaware of them, the dansers closing in. For just an instant Gwen could see the face of the seer, blind and eyeless but malignant. Not blank, not hooded, but actively evil, staring at the man, avid, greedy. Gwen spun, an extra step, fast and graceless, felt between the seer and the old man and saw in that instant his love for his wife, their house, small and cluttered, their cats, fat and spreading. They had grown children, grandchildren, had a small nest egg, guilty pleasures, ice cream despite her diabetes, an occasional potato chip despite his blood pressure. They still laughed together and slept spooned up on cold nights and—

"You can't have him!" Gwen shouted, angry, angrier than she'd been since the truck came screaming across from the wrong lane on the bridge, barriers broken, sound of screaming and tortured metal and the end of the world sound of metal and glass, exploding rubber, breaking concrete, the smell of the cop's cologne and her own vomit. The lights in her eyes that blocked out the sight of the still, still semi driver in the twisted, torn cab of the truck, the pen lights and the voices— "Clear!" And the *pain* and the thudding bone-flute rhythm of her heartbeat, the throbbing drum cadence of the blood in her body again.

"Thought we *lost* you," someone said, a voice too close to make sense, and now she thought it had been a question, malignant, ugly, a hissing voice, "Thought we *lost* you?" But she had been on the cold wet bloody asphalt, she had been trying to breathe around crushed ribs, she had been reaching even as the medics pulled back far enough for the jolts from the paddles. Reaching for the cell phone. Because it was Robert. She knew it was Robert. Calling her back as they couldn't have. "Thought we *lost* you," the medics had said.

And Gwen had reached for the cell phone that stopped ringing then. The cell phone that had startled her the instant before her car swerved and jumped the barrier, and there was the sound of air brakes and the scream of tires and the driver of the semi, unmoving in the cab. Forever unmoving.

"No."

"*We* don't lose people," the seer said.

Gwen wrenched free. Again. That bony grip. Those dry, scaly fingers. She pulled away. She pulled away. She pulled—lost, over and over, not quite back yet, hadn't Robert said something about that, still shocky, still so afraid? Danse Macabre meant death had passed you by. But what if instead you had run? What if, instead—

—and the whole week. Lost as if dreaming. She woke screaming at night. She jolted into reality by day. Caught somewhere in between, in a place where men and women in masks and robes could move through and between people who didn't sense them.

"I didn't die!" Gwen shouted, and pulled the cell from her pocket. It showed new messages, several, more coming, Robert frantically trying to reach her. She'd never felt it vibrate. Danse Macabre came closer. They walked now, the dance forgotten. Somehow worse. A threat. They were around her. "*Please*," she said and the phone in her hands rang. Gwen startled, fumbled the phone, caught it and tried to say hello.

But there was no breath in her lungs. It had been knocked out when she jolted forward, connected with the steering wheel and flew back, her neck whiplashed, cheekbone deeply bruised, her ribs crushed, hands all but broken against the steering wheel and every muscle bruised and sprained.

"We thought we'd lost you," a voice said and she forced her eyes open fast, terrified the other voice would follow. Terrified she was back here—*it's been a week, more than a week, it already happened, I lived, I lived, damn it*—

And then the phone rang again, Robert, surely Robert, and she reached for it without thinking, somewhere down around her thigh beside her on the cold, hard, wet, bloody asphalt, the medics seemingly not even phased by this and—

"She's going into arrest!" someone shouted, sound of footsteps, someone crying her name, it sounded like Robert but that was impossible, he wasn't *here*, the sound of the phone and someone yelled, "Shit!" and then, "Got it, clear!" and the pain, like lightning jumping through her ribs, the pain that sent her screaming clear of her body.

And into the clearing.

The Danse Macabre stood around her.

You cheated, the seer who had pulled her said directly into her mind. The voice was silver and cold. *You stole. He was alive when they first reached him.* The driver in the semi cab, so still. Already cold. Colder than could be explained at autopsy. As if he'd been dead for several hours. Or had the life ripped from him.

Not true. She was still herself.

"Come." Their hands out toward her. The music stilled. They stood around her, waiting.

The cell phone rang. She clutched it. Magic charm. Lifeline. *Robert.*

"No. You got your victim. If that's what you think. One lived, one died. *I'm alive.*"

The seer blurred, spun too fast to follow. Gwen squeezed her eyes closed. "He only had another week. Crank. Speed. Downers. He only had another week."

Rage makes her dizzy. "That doesn't mean *me.*"

The seer starts to speak. But a boneman steps forward in her place. "Then who? You stepped between us twice. You've chosen a proxy before. Choose now."

The sound of the voice is bamboo wind chimes rattling before a storm. She makes her choice almost without thinking. She won't be cheated again. The old man with the ice blue eyes and snow white hair is safe from her. She's given him a few more years of ice cream and stolen potato chips with his wife and children and grandchildren and those fat, fat cats. She's made her choice and the silver world around her wavers and starts to collapse, everything falling at her faster and faster, the danse around her, insanely loud and fast and she screams for Robert, the phone in her hands ringing—

"Daniel," she says, when she wants to say Robert. The phone is wrong, one of the new, flat kind, not her friendly, shorting-out flip phone. The child in her arms stirs and says, "Daddy," around a wet thumb. The body is too short and aches in unfamiliar places. Part of it is missing, removed, replaced, unnatural.

"No," Gwen says. "No."

"Jessica," says the voice on the phone. "There you are."

She recognizes it now. Daniel. Of course. She's—Jessica? *Gwen.* *What life would you take?*

No. "No," Gwen says. She didn't mean to *trade.* On the phone, Daniel laughs.

Robert stays past the close. He stays until there's no one there but staff. He stays while sheriff's deputies are called, until men with flashlights and dogs straining at leashes go into the woods, searching, calling, crashing through the underbrush. He stays until true night has fallen and receded, silver shadows lifting off the glen, individual trees appearing from the murk, twilight in reverse; dawn. He stays until Sunday officially starts, the bread baking, the coffee brewing, the Ren Faire people in bawdy costumes scatter new hay, walking around him gingerly as if they've all been briefed on the man who lost his wife.

Or his mind. Did she ever come home? Did he lose her that hateful day when she reached to answer her phone on the bridge because she knew it was him and her Bluetooth was broken and he was the only one she'd risk that ticket for, the only one to make her look away and fumble for her phone and look back up only to find—

No. She'd come home. He'd held her while she'd cried. He'd bathed her wounds and gotten her into a hot bath. He'd watched as they told him to for signs of concussion. He'd thanked every power that might be for giving her back.

And he'd spent a week with her, wondering if she'd come all the way back. A confused and confusing week with a woman who wasn't quite the same.

Robert went still, standing on the path outside the leather worker's tent, the turquoise and white tent, the last place he'd seen her. Just before the dancers came.

"Not all the way back," Robert whispered.   Danse Macabre meant death had passed you by.

He looked at his watch. The Faire was limbering up for the day. The dancers would be here soon.

I wrote The Little Cat for an anthology that was later canceled, so the story went looking for a home. It found one in the last issue of Challenging Destiny, a little 'zine I'd wanted to get a story into for years. The story was written on a sunny fall afternoon as the leaves turned and I sat outside and moved only enough to stay in the sun until the tale ended.

The Little Cat in the Attic Window,

the Blue House on the Corner

There's a big house on the corner lot, the kind of house that looks like it should be broken up into apartments. Three stories plus a basement, kitchen in the back, trees crowding the front porch and, in one instance, shoving it upward. The house is blue and white, but an old, faded, teal-ish blue, turquoise almost, something that looks dead and flat at night. The oak in the front yard drops acorns all around the porch and the upper branches strain for the roof, one of those smushed-point roofs, kind of an *Amityville Horror* house look to it and in the attic there are a couple of round windows and one of those arched top, flat bottomed ones.

That's where the little cat sits. Jess sees him in the mornings when she's walking to work. He sits on the southeast side, morning sunlight picking out his fine long springy whiskers; at night when she walks home he's lying in the southwest sun, content and squinty-eyed. Little brown cat with stripes and she doesn't know why she assumes he's a boy, she just does.

Lately Jess finds she's anticipating the cat. Like he's a friend of hers. Like she'll stop and they'll chat and he'll ask her what she has planned for the day when she passes by in the morning and in the evening he'll ask how her day went.

He's someone else's cat, she reminds herself, but she still looks forward to seeing him and he hasn't let her down yet.

When Jess gets home in the evenings she checks messages and mail and voice mail and email accounts and there's never anything there. Well, there is, of course—there's email from the lists she's on and snail mail from her various pen pals across the country and usually there's even a call or two, reminders of appointments or offers of merchandise or even her own voice, reminding her of some task, some necessity. But there's never anything from anyone she really cares about. It's like her first onion circle is empty. Onions peel out from the core in layers, layer upon layer, each one out that much farther from the center. That's how Jess feels about relationships. Everyone has that first onion circle, that immediate circle of people who mean more than anything, the ones most near and dear, the ones to do anything for, the ones to die without.

Hers is empty. No one there. No one home. Just Jess and the feeling that something is missing. Just Jess and the thought of someone else's cat. She daydreams about it, dreams about it. At night she dreams she lives in a big gray house (or blue?) with a man who loves her so much he'd do anything for her, anything at all if she'd just tell him. A man who loves her so much she can almost hear him say her name and she wakes trembling on the edge of something, some knowledge or discovery or truth, but she wakes alone to another day.

She came here because it's a big California city, temperate and sprawling, big enough to get lost in, with enough people, places and things she was sure she could start a new life.

I *have*, she thinks fiercely, but it's meant leaving everyone and everything else behind. And sometimes she can't remember who she's left behind and sometimes she's not sure there's anyone left behind at all, or that there was ever anyone there to begin with.

In the summer Jess walked every day to work with no one and nothing and she watched couples and families and even single people on the streets and everyone looked content or purposeful or fulfilled or at least alive and Jess had to dodge out of their way when they came towards her. Even when there were people and traffic near her the hot morning air felt sullen and secretive, excluding her somehow, as if she were not a part of the city. Every morning she walked to work in a quiet bookstore where the owner rarely spoke or even emerged from behind his stack of books. With the coming of winter she took a second job on her days off, this one in a children's bookstore, loud voices and kinetic motion and mothers brimming with love and umbrage, but none of it coming Jess's way. She tried to talk to the mothers but they constantly interrupted her with prohibitions to the children and when they looked courteously back at her she'd try again until this time the mother would interrupt Jess herself or be interrupted by her offspring and sometimes the mothers would tell their children to go to the play area and wait, but then Jess would lose track of her conversational gambit and stutter to a halt, or forget what she'd meant to say at all, or just feel too intimidated to try again.

She tried talking to the children, sometimes, but that made the mothers nervous.

In the evenings she took a job waiting tables in a small, trendy hangout actually within walking distance of her apartment and there she found loud and vibrant conversations and jokes and insults and laughter but all of it swirled around her and left her on her own little island, untouched, and she learned for the first time that no one actually sees the server. Even when she was somehow part of a joke, when someone included her in a tease or invited her in by rolling his eyes or asking her opinion, still by the time the check was paid and the coats were collected, those people had moved on and they no longer saw her as anything but their way out.

Jess sometimes took to walking home on an alternate route to avoid the blue house and the little cat because they made her more lonely than ever and the house was more faded and farther back from the road every day and

everything seemed gray. But in the morning there was only one sensible way to go to work, and that took her directly by the house.

When Jess walks to work in the morning the little cat meows at her would feel like to have him come running up to greet her at the door, soft winding around her legs and enthusiastic purring as she picks him up. At least one person would know she was alive. In the evening Jess walks home from the bookstore, or maybe from the restaurant, her days are starting to blur a bit. But she's tired and so takes the direct route home and when she passes the blue house on the corner she notices it looks ramshackle and unkempt, the grass needs cutting, the paint is flaking, the windows are cloudy. In the upstairs window the little cat meows at her and paws at the window as she goes by, dark little paw pads pressed against the glass. He's insistent and Jess feels the first thrill of fear that something is wrong. She stops and stands and watches him but in the end she walks away. He's a cat, after all. Just being a cat. Maybe there was a fly in the window or something.

In the morning the little cat is even more insistent and Jess, now afraid, stops moving and stares up at him. The house seems sad to her, shut down, in mourning or lost. Maybe something has happened to the people in the house. Maybe they've fallen ill or gone off on a short trip and failed to return or the cat sitter forgot to come. Maybe they've gone off and forgotten they live there.

That's crazy, she tells herself, but in the attic window the cat is in fits trying to get to her and Jess looks around furtively as if she's about to commit a heinous crime and lets herself in through the front gate.

No one answers her nervous knocking, no one responds when she calls out and Jess falls silent, watching the front door, partly as if she expects something is about to happen she didn't cause, partly knowing what she's about to do.

The door is unlocked. The knob feels cool and smooth and familiar under her hand. She holds her breath as she steps inside, no longer calling. Her heart trembles and she tells herself it's just anticipation. She tells herself she's just checking on the welfare of the cat. In the state where she used to live there was a statute that people could do just about anything to rescue an animal. She doesn't know if that's the case where she is now.

She steps into the entrance and closes the door.

Inside the house is sun warm and light and airy. Hardwood floors, deep green walls leading lighter and lighter into the house, and she knows where every room is, every stick of furniture. She knows the smell of breakfast cooking and the sound her shoes make on the floor.

The little cat comes bounding to greet her. He rubs against her legs, purring, ecstatic. He meows up at her and she laughs and picks him up; he seems inordinately heavy.

She wanders farther into the house. Her heart has stopped pounding and she feels curiously at ease, becoming lighter and lighter as she walks, cat in her arms and she's obviously trespassing but she feels more at home than she's can remember feeling in ages.

Living room, drawing room, somebody's office—maybe Eric's? Eric. The name resonates. Dining room, breakfast nook, kitchen. Up the stairs and it's as if she's drawn, moving along the front hallway to a room where a woman lies in a huge oak framed bed. The room's on the front of the house and faces south and sunlight streams through the windows. The woman is surrounded, connected to living machines, tubes and monitors and moving graphs and her eyes are closed, her chest barely moves, she's so far away Jess has to squint to see her at all but she's familiar somehow, someone she's seen before and there's a man in the room, he moves suddenly and Jess backs up a step but all his attention is on the woman in the bed.

The cat snuggles tight under her chin, constant rumble of purr, and the man brushes one hand over his face, a gesture of despair as he looks at the woman in the bed, the woman he loves so much he'd do anything for her, anything at all if she'd just tell him.

Jess takes another step back and the cat flies from her arms, jumps to the bed to knead the woman's legs through the blankets. The man makes an abrupt move toward them but the woman opens her eyes, slowly, as if not used to doing so, and says in a thin, tired voice, "I had the most curious dream that everything I loved was gone, that I was alone and lost within the city and no one could see me—"

He reaches for her, and the cat meows, and Jess feels herself sliding and slipping, disappearing and becoming thin and stretched like a dream at the edge of waking. The little cat stands on her legs in the bed while Jess slips and slides and winds down back inside and opens her eyes and comes home.

The Return was written at Clarion Writers Workshop during a very hot Midwestern summer.

The Return

In the strong sunlight that filled the world that afternoon, the ghost seemed almost nothing, insubstantial, its being diminished until there was almost nothing of the specter to see and feel and fear. In the strong sunlight of that last glorious late summer afternoon, there was nothing to fear, nothing at all. October brought storms, though. November dropped thunder and lightning into endless sleet that slanted down the corridors of steely afternoons and dank evenings. December was a time-out, holiday lights and brightly wrapped packages that drove away the fear of my nights alone. I could sleep as long as two or three hours at a stretch.

Until January came, cold and slow with crows crying through the long evenings. In those short days and long, slow, frozen nights, the ghost returned, stalking the house after sundown, lingering after dawn, darkening the afternoons. I walked afraid of the future.

Adam left during January, saying I had changed. When I walked the house, I saw his shadow; when I sat quiet, I heard his voice. But the nights were long and though the house was empty, it was not empty enough. I learned to avoid mirrors. I walked the edges of rooms with my back to the walls. I tucked my feet in close to me when I sat, holding myself together. I drew in slowly, falling inward, protecting myself, but I was already too late and likely had been all along.

During the days, I worked out of the office in the main house, my uncle's house, running the charitable foundation his will had set up, overseeing the distribution of funds and the remodeling of the gatehouse where I lived. I hoped to draw in other benefactors and drive out the coldness I felt, but even as spring approached my own heart refused to thaw. Adam was gone and it was a lonely spring of ice and rot. In the mirrors at night, I watched myself to see what remained behind my eyes.

Firelight warmed the main house walls in reds and golds. Outside, late December wound down. Our feet were propped too close on the hearth, Dave's socks giving off a scorched cotton smell and my own bare feet prickling and twitching from the heat, rubbing against each other. Neither of us wanted to move. A plate of out-of-season grapes, and cheese and bread, lay untouched on the end table and we held glasses of deep red wine that tasted sour but winked rubies in the firelight. Dave's arm across my shoulder was warm.

"What are you doing tomorrow?" I asked lazily, running one foot up the side of his. His white socks were burning hot.

"Bookstore," Dave answered. His voice held a sleepy tone. "Work." He leaned his head down to mine and rubbed his cheek over my hair. "Nothing interesting, Jessica."

Outside the wind had picked up and in the fireplace the flames flickered higher, sparking on damp wood. I moved closer against him. Never felt as if I could get close enough, somehow make us one. I felt Dave stiffen and I held my breath. A moment later he relaxed, his hip soft against mine again but his arm no longer around me. I snuggled into him and hooked my arm through his. "Can you meet me for lunch?" Again, that hesitation before he agreed. He asked me about my day, more foundation work, tracking the charities, getting grant papers together for the board review, contacting organizations for donations, making calls, doing mailings.

Since the time Adam had left, life had fallen into a comfortable pattern, but it had taken work. Now the days in the gatehouse and the main house revolved around foundation work and Dave, days of meetings and business and evenings of passion, but still he hadn't asked for anything more. I sighed. The pattern worked well. In the evenings the crows would watch as we came and went from the gatehouse at the edge of the property, their calls smug.

It had taken me months to draw someone into my life and I faced each day with the fear that he would leave me and the ghost would return, filling each day with the special terror she had reserved for me. Walking into a room I would jolt at my own image reflected from a mirror. My heart would pound and my head would feel light. After many minutes I'd return to normal, facing myself in the looking glass, reminding myself that Dave and I had hung the mirror ourselves, had moved it from its original place and that it did not come here to haunt me but waited in the spot that I had left it out of respect, or immobility. My image in the mirror would remain consistent and dull, unchanging. I liked it that way. When my courage returned I would turn my head this way and that, looking for terrors that had once lurked beneath my skin. Sometimes Dave would come in and find me and laugh and tease me out of the mood until any danger of haunting seemed utterly past.

"I'm going to start dinner," I said, rising at last. I stood facing Dave where he sat on the couch. My feet were instantly cold. December was sliding into January and the house bled warmth into the frozen countryside, but was warmer than the gatehouse, so we spent many evenings there.

"Want any help?" Dave asked in a sleepy voice that was far from being an actual offer.

I laughed and nudged him with my foot. "I think I can make spaghetti without you," I said and Dave rolled his eyes and whined.

"Spaghetti, again?"

"You want to come help me with something else?"

Dave closed his eyes. "Mmm," he said. "Spaghetti, again."

I think he was asleep before I left the room, which is why I didn't scream when I hit the hallway. The little pile of bones was obscene against the clean wood floor and white walls, the fur ragged and bloody, the tail torn from the little gray body.

I dropped and pressed my hands hard against my mouth while a scream built somewhere deep inside me. Poor little thing – poor little thing – Reaching out to gather it up and carry it sadly into the kitchen, through to the back porch where it would freeze and remain until I could bury it or until one of the crows carried it off. The fur under my fingers was still soft, the little feet pink and perfect.

I trembled on the porch. My breath steamed around me like something separate from me and alive. I'd been afraid she would return, afraid the ghost would find me.

The next night we slid from one year to the next, and Dave made love to me as the clock struck the hour and the new year began, but he did not ask me to marry him. He hadn't, not on Christmas Eve, or Christmas, and he wouldn't on Valentine's day. I was afraid he would leave as the others had, slipping away quietly in the night, content to leave behind their possessions if it meant being quit of me. Disappeared, as completely and utterly as if they had never been. Sometimes then I would find a little pile of bones and fur, and cry and bury them. And sometimes I would find larger piles, of bones, and skin.

January was full of ice and fury. On calmer days teachers brought children to fill the houses with their light and excitement, their high piping voices filling the empty spaces as they clamored through my uncle's halls. He had been a big game hunter before he turned conservationist and the main house still held numerous trophies, a tiger pelt from India, elephant tusks from Africa. Once the stuffed head of an orangutan had hung over the fireplace to alarm visitors but that had been removed years ago by very popular demand.

He had lived a long life and died with a to do list on his bedside table. *Give back* topped the list. Charles started the foundation because of Claire. His baby sister, beloved childhood friend, grew to adulthood while Charles was away in the service. He returned home to find her utterly changed, coldly vicious. No longer a child of light, Claire had grown into a young woman of anger and fury, who tormented animals and left a string of lovers behind her. She was barely 20 when she killed her last lover and only my uncle's money would have kept her from the asylum if Claire hadn't thrown herself to her death from the roof of the main house on New Year's Day, 1947.

The foundation had come out of Claire's tragedy, good coming out of sorrow, Charles Trelane using his father's money to reclaim Claire's memory as he could not reclaim her soul.

January was full of good days that year, cold but clear, with field trips and grant requests and I spent the days busy. I spent the days giving, free to spend Charles' money, to the extent the board allowed. That meant working with children and animals and artists. I got to tour a petting and breeding zoo, walk a new wing of a children's hospital where artists were routinely brought in to teach. I awarded a grant to a new little theater and another no-kill animal shelter. And at one point during the month I got to hold a pair of baby owls, downy and warm and snugly, cupped in my hands, their tiny hearts racing against their feathered breasts. I spent some days in my office in the main house with the Royale typewriter and the ornately curled name plate on the desk, the front of it reading "Claire." The nights I spent alone with David, happy and almost secure.

Until the deep winter night when Dave phoned from the city. He had been detained on business and with the roads the way they were, couldn't see himself driving home. In truth I couldn't either, though a small, selfish part of me wished he would try. I kept him talking as long as I could, a call full of broken snaps and poppings as the line between us muttered and protested the cold. At last we said our good nights and I tried to picture with sympathy Dave alone in his office trying to make the best of the situation, working late and sleeping on the couch in the lounge. But my mind betrayed me, sending up pictures of voluptuous secretaries and four poster beds. It was one a.m. before my eyes closed in sleep.

Less than an hour later the scream sent me straight up in bed, heart pounding for release, adrenaline spiking.

The scream was mine.

I ran, no thought but to get out. I ran through the main house to the front door and jerked it open but the night and the blizzard and the gale winds drove me back and slammed the door out of my hands and into the wall. The carpet in front of me was instantly soaked, snow starting to stick to the rug. I grabbed the door and tried to force it closed and all the time I heard the sound of crying all around me. I backed away from the door, into the living room, afraid, trying to figure out where to go. When I turned back into the room, the mirror across from me reflected black, deep and shifting. I could not see myself in the reflection. Something started to waver in the glass and I bolted. I made my way upstairs to find my shoes, my clothes. I thought my 4x4 would make it through the snow. If it didn't, at least I was out of the house. Whatever was here, it had tried to claim me before, when Adam had left. I would not remain to give it another chance.

I passed the mirror on my way out and risked one last look. Damnation danced across its depths, the face within it a terror of burning fear, and not mine.

I ran without looking back.

The café was small and rundown, the kind of place that patches the worn sections in the greasecloth plaid table covers. But tonight candleflame lit my table as I huddled in the corner of the booth, both hands wrapped around a rapidly cooling cup of coffee, the last I had gotten just before the power cut out and the ice-filled gale began to hammer at the windows.

The phones were out when I tried to call Dave's office, but when I picked up the handset it was filled with a low and ugly laughter that sent me spinning away, my hands pressed tightly against my mouth. Cell service was down too.

When I surfaced from my thoughts, the waitress was kneeling in the booth next to mine. Initially I thought she was praying and thought about joining her. I'm not ordinarily religious, but too many months on a haunted estate has an effect. The waitress was not praying, however; she was searching the night outside the window and now she dropped back down to the seat and turned to me.

"There's somebody out there," she said. "I think it's a dog." Her teeth were smeared with purple lipstick. Her eye makeup had been scrubbed off by tired hands. She looked about 12. It took me a minute to make out what she'd just said and then I didn't believe her.

"Can't be. No one could survive this night," I said, and knelt up on my own bench. The waitress – her nametag read "Erin" – pulled the curtain back and pointed. Outside, a single ice-caked figure flailed in the swirling snow and blistering ice winds. Even as I watched, the figure – human – went down on one knee, dropping as if too exhausted to go on.

The other diners included two very old men, a mother and her toddler, and the waitress. There was no one else and I certainly couldn't leave someone out there in that storm. Back into the screaming explosion of night and sound. The figure in front of me had fallen again, and this time was lying flat against the windblown white ground that shifted and slipped beneath my feet. Suddenly the figure looked like Dave and I found myself trying to run, floundering across the slick surface, breath panting in and out and it wasn't until I got close enough to the figure that it was too late to return to the relative warmth and safety of the diner that I realized my mistake.

The white figure turned and grinned out of my eyes and snarling teeth. The ghost from the mirror.

I reached out, meaning to drive her back, but instead my hands caught her shoulders and she came closer. The next instant there was nothing in front of me, no one there, but inside I was crowded. I could feel the change, someone pushing me aside, hemming me in, cramming up against me, sending me backwards and smaller as though I suffocated, air tearing against my chest, but my heart not pumping it through. In terror I began to thrash, feeling strong hands suddenly on my shoulders, dragging me upright. The cook, I guessed – there were white pants sticking out from under the coat he wore. The waitress was with him, the two of them staring at me, shaking me, their mouths opening and closing but the storm tore away their voices, the wind tore away their words. Inside, I tore away from my grip on the soul.

Jessica's soul.

Silence for a moment. Then nothing. An instant of almost non-existence. Again. And then the screaming horror of the ghost, too long denied these last 13 months as she screams her terror back into me. She screams her way back into her soul and my grip gives way completely. I slide, ripping free, and free fall. Out of her body. Tumbling lost within the storm and Jessica's anger follows me. It's been her face in the mirror all this time, not my face as I remembered it from all those years ago but her face, naked without the overlay of the body I wore. The body I had stolen. In a last moment of shared consciousness, I see her looking at me, see me looking at her, the two of us kneeling in the blizzard with our hands braced against each other. The cook and the waitress stand shouting, their words lost and torn away. They cannot see me now, only her. Only Jessica. No Claire. Jessica is home again and I am lost and tumbling away and the storm shrieks against me for one last moment before there is darkness.

In the white darkness, I am reborn. I am no ghost, haunting myself. In the darkness, I send Claire flying. I reclaim my being. I reclaim my soul. In the whiteness, I promise myself the future.

In the dark stormlight of the winter night, Claire's ghost seems almost nothing, and my soul everything.

The Book of Halves started as a free writing exercise during lunch with a fantastic writer and fantastic friend. After writing the first couple pages as exercise in a five minute rush, I read it to Sue, who said, "What happens next?"

The Book of Halves

Grimoire, the title read, and Jill plucked it from the moldering stack instantly, turned to Nick to say, "Look what I've found!" and discovered he'd wandered off into some other part of the store. A delightful store, all dust motes, sunlight and redwood walls, sun beaming through skylights into the narrow bookcrowded aisles. The books were old, worm-ridden, threatening to send bookworms into home collections but the titles were irresistible: A True History of Angels. The War in Heaven. Prophecies of Zeus. Satan: Therapy and Revenge. And a little further over, between a giddy mass market witch's spell book and a Colin Wilson occult tome, she found the grimoire, a book of two halves, and finding Nicky had wandered away, dropped crossed-legged to the dusty water-spotted carpet and began to read. The first half was one thing, but the second half was dark, not the white magic grimoire of angels but the deep purply black of demons crying and leathery wings. She flipped through the pages of the Book of Halves, looking again for the light.

"Are you ready to go?"

The book flew out of her hands Jill jolted so hard and she scrambled on the filthy bookshop floor as if it were vitally important she catch the volume before it dropped. She did, barely, her arms outstretched on the scratchy rug and she pulled the book to her with sweaty hands.

"I didn't mean to scare you," Nick said, reaching for her hands to pull her up.

"Half to death," Jill said and looked up through the skylight directly over them. The sky had gone completely black. "How long have we been here?"

Nick laughed like she was joking. "It's a thunderstorm," he said. "Is that all you found? I'm getting off cheap for a change."

Jill nodded and followed him down narrow wooden stairs to the cashier by the front door and with every step she heard his words repeat – *I'm getting off cheap* – and thought somehow he was wrong.

The storm rolled into their city and set up camp.

Jill and Nick ran for the car while overhead lightning sketched the glowering sky into purple negatives. Wind caught the trees, streetlights throwing shadows of wildly waving branches. Thunder boomed, fell away muttering as rain begin to fall thick and hard.

In the car they hauled out treasures from recycled grocery bags, Nick's westerns, war histories, something on fashion from the 50s and she so didn't want to ask why, thrillers, mysteries, a huge and tattered bestseller now three years out of date, The History of Angels that had so intrigued her, a book on puppies that made Jill raise her eyebrows and, at the bottom, the Book of Halves.

They both went still when Jill pulled it out of the bag, as if their feeding frenzy of books had abruptly ended. There was only the hard drumming downpour on metal and the wavelike sound of water racing across the dry desert parking lot.

Jill held the thing rather reverently. It wasn't until she looked away from the battered leather book that she saw Nick's appreciation didn't match hers. He'd moved back in the car, as if away from her. His eyes were worried, his mouth set as if he smelled something impolite in an extremely polite social setting.

Before she could ask he said, "I don't like that. I know something about these things, Jill. They're dangerous. I knew someone who – who got hurt with one of these. This isn't a good idea. Where did you even get it?"

Jill stared at her husband and best friend, the man she spent hours rock climbing and booking and eating and sleeping with, the man she could tell anything to and loved more than any other ever, and felt a furious stab of something like hatred or jealousy or rage. Or all of those.

Above all, she felt the need to protect. She pressed the book against her chest with her arms around it. The old black leather felt worn, warm and soft. "Well, I like it," she said softly, facing forward into the black pre-night of streaming rain.

Nick started the car and drove them home instead of the movie and dinner they had planned.

Calling Angels. But the script was dark and heavy, the runes harsh and hard. The pages under Jill's fingers felt soft and thick, velvety. When she took her hands away the pages left a crumbling dust on her hands.

The book lay across her lap. Watery moonlight touched the pages. She'd laid in bed beside Nick as long as she could, listening to his easy breathing, taking what comfort she could from his warmth and closeness.

When she got up, Nicky stretched one hand toward her. His face in sleep contorted. She thought if he'd been awake he'd try to stop her, and she'd felt a sudden savage joy. He wasn't awake.

He couldn't stop her from going after the grimoire.

Early autumn. The wood floor under her feet was cold. The storm had ended some time earlier. The book felt warm and buttery under her fingers. It fit in her hand, the way some pieces of clothing or accessories fit, feeling right. She'd left it in the loft, an impromptu library just outside their master suite, kind of a waste of space at the top of the stairs the developers had tried to turn into a selling point rather than a design flaw. "Loft," they'd said about what was really an oversized landing with a half-wall. For Jill and Nick, it was a library.

Halfway down the stairs she stopped on the window seat beside the tall, tall window that really was a selling point. She'd only come this far because she'd heard Nick moving restlessly when she was in the loft. Here the streetlight and moonlight illuminated the pages through the many small panes of the window, no need for artificial light, no reason to alert Nick to her sneaking around –

I'm not sneaking around, I just couldn't sleep and he can –

– here she could read. Here she could look out over the living room and past the breakfast bar into the kitchen, seeing most of it under the cabinets. It really was a small home, but it worked for them.

Sitting here, she could see the pages.

Calling angels. But the words were in such harsh black letters. Such a strong hand. As if someone had written out the grimoire when only this afternoon surely it had been printed?

"I don't believe in angels," Jill whispered. She didn't believe in any of this stuff, had gotten it out of the sheerest curiosity, and the edge of fear *what if* could engender.

She guessed she wanted to believe there was something out there. Something more than a life where she was a paralegal and Nick ran a roofing company. She loved her life. But sometimes she just wanted something – more.

"Or different," Jill said aloud into the dark house. In her lap the soft creamy pages seemed to glow up at her. She smoothed one hand over a page and whispered the first word as if she had spoken Latin forever.

Something shifted. A chunk of night-dark house, a square of it, moved, as if someone had cut a photograph of the living room and moved a piece of the picture somewhere else. No, a negative. Jill squinted and hunched forward on the window seat. She saw clear reality in the living room, straight lines, clean edges. And she saw room superimposed on room, like looking through a film of a room at the same room, the two subtly off from each other, the overlay uneven and imperfect.

What the hell? Jill thought but opened her mouth and clearly said the second word.

The room shifted. Another square appeared, this one over the light that hung the distance from the cathedral ceiling to just over the front door. She had a clear image of the transom window over the door, the lower part of the frosted glass light, and through the image, subtly off, the reality of the light, the window, the top of the door. The next words came fast, her voice low but not a whisper. Cold air brushed her neck from the tall window behind her.

Latin words rolled like water on her tongue. Half a dozen more windows opened and she caught her breath, heart pounding too fast. Whatever was happening, it made no sense. It wasn't wonderful or awful, it was just –

"Different," she breathed and stared into the night dark living room at the windows there, each a little off, maybe showing different times, or different realities. She let go of the book and rubbed her eyes with both hands. Nothing. It could so easily be nothing, it's nothing, it's–

The book on her lap slipped. She caught it with a hard jolt, hands tight and protective and the next words came fast in a low growl. Windows proliferated. They stacked over each other. She looked through them like looking through stacks of playing cards standing on end, fanned slightly to one side, and through each she saw something different, and everything she saw was wonderful. Everything she saw was something lost and now found again – friends who had moved away, relatives and animals who had died, homes she had loved, her favorite bedroom as a child, the oak tree her father had cut down. Laurie. Precious, lost Laurie. And in windows over the other windows, she saw things changing. The oak tree tall and growing, but the house around it neglected and damaged. Animals returned as if from the grave but new friendships trounced and lost forever. Everything glowed with such joy and light, but everything came with a price, she thought. But maybe the price wasn't too much. Because the joy *shined*. The windows – worlds – opened faster and faster, worlds within worlds filling the cathedral ceiling and the living room, thick with light and she thought she could see figures in the light, as if she looked at –

I don't believe in angels –

– faces of joy. The living room burned with pure white flame, worlds and joy and chances.

Nick slapped her so hard her neck cracked as her head rocked back. For an instant she saw past him, still into the flickering abyss and the faces – twisted – and forms – brutal – and the nightmares that would never end, never allow solace and –

I don't believe in demons she screamed and the world – all of the worlds – fell away.

The coffee was too hot. She kept burning her mouth on it. The kitchen was full of some kind of mist, surreal and interesting.

No. She shook her head, causing too hot coffee to splash onto her fingers, burning her again. Smoke. The kitchen was full of smoke. That was not unusual. That was Sunday morning routine and Nick trying to cook breakfast, determined that someday he'd get it right. Privately, Jill doubted it. It seemed to her that after all these years of trying if he hadn't figured out that oven mitts left on a hot burner would catch on fire, he wasn't gonna, and she thought maybe not catching things on fire was the first step to making edible – french toast?

"Fire," she said thickly. Ought to stand and do something about it but Nicky was right there, handy glass of OJ.

"That stinks."

She closed her eyes and nodded. In a few more minutes he'd run out of eggs and take her out to breakfast. Wherever he wanted to take her was fine. They were bound to have better coffee. She needed that. Didn't feel like she'd slept at all.

"That was one hell of a dream you had last night," Nicky said, and put the rest of the eggs back in the fridge.

"Dream?"

"You dreamed something about." He broke off and looked at her like he suddenly didn't remember. "Angels. Or. Demons. Something." His eyebrows came together and he looked more upset than not remember a dream of hers – which she couldn't remember at all – was more important than it actually was.

"Are you sure it wasn't your dream?"

He nodded slowly. "Could be. Maybe." He took an inefficient swipe at the stove where the fire had gone out and the smoke still rose. "Do you want to go–"

"I thought you'd never ask."

"Sometimes I think you don't like my cooking," Nicky said with mock despair.

"Sometimes?" Jill asked.

Midmorning, Jill sat in a spill of sunlight downstairs while Nick, upstairs, showered. She'd wanted some time alone. To read, to figure out what was nagging her, or whatever the opposite of nagging was. A sensation that something wonderful was about to happen, or had just happened, or had been promised. Something coming.

Something almost there.

A stray beam of sunlight caught one of the panes of glass in the tall window and made it glow. Then the sun slipped a little further up in the sky and most of the panes went opaque, each slightly different from the one next to it. The living room dipped under her. Before she even caught her balance she made her way to the stairs and stumbled halfway up.

The window seat was covered by a thick cushion, deep blue, something she'd made when they first moved in, and wedged behind it, between the pillow and the window, was a chunk of light. It was gold. It was old. It was wonderful.

"I must not have gotten any sleep. How could I have forgotten?" She held the book tight in both hands, eyes scanning the cover. The book was soft, battered leather, golden words, angelic script and she couldn't remember what was still nagging at her, something from the night before – hadn't Nicky said she had a dream? – but whatever it was, it was wonderful, like a wonderful dream, the kind that makes the entire next day a little brighter.

She just kept thinking about Laurie, so close again, like they'd been in high school and all the way through college, up to that hideous moment when there'd been such sudden light and the slamming and the flying million pieces of light that resolved into the shattered, refracting windshield and Laurie's face, stilled into a grimace of horror, the last thing Jill would ever see of her friend. She'd been in the hospital during Laurie's funeral and Laurie's parents would never have let Jill come.

They blamed her.

She blamed herself. But the anticipation she had today didn't fade. She could feel Laurie, as if the phone was just about to ring. Or the shower would turn off and instead of Nick it would be her best friend emerging, like when they'd been roommates, same as she'd always been, a little plump, silly, grinning. Maybe a little tipsy.

The water turned off in the shower and Jill went upstairs without another thought. She left the grimoire tucked just under the cushion on the window seat. Not really hidden, but Nicky didn't like it, so why subject him to it?

The bedroom was full of light. The nearest neighbors were far enough away they didn't have to pull the curtains in the daylight. She could just see Nicky through the pall of steam in the bathroom. He seemed far away. Distant. The image didn't even make her blink. Something good was going to happen. She bounced on the bed and waited for Nick, her t-shirt and pants joining the pile of laundry from the day before. She slid under the covers before he came out of the bathroom, peered at him over the edge of the sheet, playful till she got a look at his face.

She sat up fast, frowning. The bedroom suddenly seemed cold. Cold air pressed against her back and made her shiver.

"What's wrong?"

He sat on the edge of the bed and ran a hand over his clean shaven face. For a minute he seemed confused, then he shook his head and grinned at her. It wasn't convincing. "Just a little -- dizzy," but he said it like that wasn't quite it. "And a little headache." He shook his head again, like driving away a persistent fly. Or convincing himself. "I'm sure it's nothing. But would you mind if we-- ?"

They linked their arms around each other. She'd never seen another couple cuddle that way, not in movies or on TV, anyway. But they usually lay together in a hug, her head more on his biceps than chest or shoulder. She was superstitious. Hearing his heart beat made her afraid it would stop. Nicky was older than her, quite a bit, and his idea of working out was parking at the far end of a parking lot and walking to whatever building he was going to.

Under the covers with the late morning sunlight pouring in, the room was warm again, but Jill was still cold.

Late in the afternoon Nick ran errands and went out to mow the lawn. Jill, taking a load of discarded socks and shoes from the living room up to the bedroom was waylaid at the window seat, where she flipped on the stair lights and sat with the book on the cushion in front of her, hands smoothing the pages as she read. Such a beautiful book, with stained glass-type illios along the edges and ornate first letters on each page. The angelic script seemed almost illuminated as she thumbed through the book, looking at a little bit here, reading a little bit there.

Understanding the Hours.

Calling the Angels.

Calming the Winds.

Healing the Ill.

Calling the Dead.

She jolted, looked again, but the page said nothing of the sort, not even close, and the dreadful brownish ink she'd thought she'd seen was gone. "You're jumpy," she told herself, but her fingers moved over the page where she thought she'd seen the impossible. *If only.* She'd missed Laurie so bad all these years. The pain of losing her had mixed with the pain of guilt, the fear she'd somehow been more responsible than everyone thought.

For just a couple more minutes she sat with one hand on the grimoire. Then from outside she heard the lawnmower go off and she stood, dropped the book and said, "That's crazy. And you know it. Dead is dead and you're lucky she didn't take you with her."

Laundry. Living room. She had dinner to figure out. On second thought, she swept the grimoire up with the load of socks and shoes and left it in the loft library stacks on her way into the bedroom, just one more book atop one of the precipitous piles.

Moonlight stretched long across the bedroom floor from the eastern window. She couldn't have been asleep long.

What woke me?

But even then Nick gave another groan and tossed from side to side.

Oh.

He was the best bed partner she'd ever had but he was far from the most restful. Nick spent his nights in balletic display, aerial feats, operatic heights. Jill had learned fast to fall asleep first, but she didn't always stay there.

The room was far colder than it should be for early fall. She reached for her bathrobe but instead found a plush jacket. That would work. Nick shot out a hand and patted her several times, as if congratulating her for something. Jill smiled a little. When they first got together she'd spent every night convinced he was dying from something violent. The truly unfair thing was he woke every morning refreshed.

The floor creaked as she crossed it. A truss snapped as the house cooled. The doorknob clacked loudly as she closed the door behind her. Nick would be oblivious.

When she turned back to the loft, it was already there. Everything had started without her and Jill moved through aching winter cold to the half wall and stared down into the living room where window after window hung like panes of slightly frosted glass, showing her different worlds. The grimoire felt like velvet in her hands, warm against the freezing night. Her feet ached on the floor. She wanted the comfort of the window seat, a halfway place neither here nor there and maybe it wouldn't be so cold with her feet tucked up under her and the jacket pulled tight. Something in the pocket bumped against her hip but she ignored it, put the book on her knees. It seemed to give off heat. She held her hands over it, laughing, and the moon had gone behind a cloud or slid up over the roof line, because she couldn't see the book, she'd have to get up and turn on the lights because there wasn't enough moonlight.

But the pages glowed when she pulled back the cover and the runes and the sigils and the words stood out stark and plain. She whispered and the worlds in the living room shifted. So many worlds and possibilities, something like 30 now, tall shards of glass, oblong, frosted, hanging from the cathedral ceiling, just far enough off from each other to show, like petals on a flower.

Worlds, she thought. And time. Lost worlds.

One of the portals showed her mother, but Jill's mother lived in Florida and smoked more cigarettes than any sane person and refused to die or even get sick from it. Not lost. She wasn't lost. Impatient, Jill rifled the pages of the grimoire without looking, her eyes searching through the worlds. Under her hands things moved in the book, something like she imagined it would feel if thick worms crawled under the pages she stroked.

"Come on," she whispered, then something in Latin, she didn't recognize it and she hadn't read it. Just knew the word and said it aloud, and then, "Laurie."

The ceiling cracked. The sound was sharp and dry, like brittle wood breaking. Several of the portals shot upwards in bursts of blinding light. Sunrise seemed to burst across the ceiling, stricken colors of rose, salmon and gold. Images rained down, broken shards and shatters of worlds. She saw pets, friends, houses, cars, everything past her, the air in the living room dead and gray as if a spark had been lost. Jill reached one hand out toward the room, into the maelstrom. "*Wait.*" She'd thought–

The book on her knees felt like it was burning. She wanted to bat it off, wanted to cry out in pain. She looked away from the swirling living room.

Blood red ink, shining against the page.

Waking the Dead.

The cell phone in the jacket pocket rang.

Suddenly she was too terrified to answer it. It vibrated in her hand and the incoming caller ID displayed a number she knew, one she'd never forgotten, had called every day for how many years? But they no longer lived there, Laurie's parents, they'd moved, couldn't stand to stay in that same house with the big oak tree in the back yard (Laurie's back yard, the oak tree was there, her father hadn't cut it down, it had just stopped being a part of Jill's life, how could she have forgotten that? How could she have confused a primal part of her own life?) The phone shrilled again, red sound against the stillness and she looked away and out at the living room where infinite worlds pulsed and burst and shattered against the reality she'd called them to. At her feet, the grimoire burned, pages flaring with light, never burning away. The sigils glowed.

From upstairs she heard Nick, his voice so small and sick.

"Stop it!" Jill yelled. Her voice was shrill and weak. "Nick?"

"Help me."

She tried to stand and the stairs shook violently, a halfway place between two worlds, or infinite possible words. She remembered the furious joy she'd felt when Nick couldn't interrupt her. This was the flip side of that – she couldn't get to him. "I'm coming!"

Answer the phone. It rang repeatedly in her hands. Maybe that was the way to make it all stop.

She couldn't say the name.

"Hello?"

"I want to come home," Laurie said. "I want to come home, Jill, it's horrible here. You have to understand. You have to bring me back."

"It wasn't my fault," Jill said slowly. Laurie was still talking, crying, babbling. Jill could feel her old friend reaching out, almost a physical presence over the slim cell phone. "It wasn't. I was drunk too. And I said call a cab. And you kept insisting. And I thought – I thought you deserved it, to get in some trouble, because you were always so perfect."

She stopped, because Laurie had stopped, and because she had to get to Nick. But there was a pressure against her, like waves, or wind, shoving her back.

"It *was* your fault!" Laurie screamed.

Jill stood. The pressure around her eased a little. "I thought so. And part of it was. But you made the final decision. You took the keys from me. You drove." A trade off. A scary ride in Laurie's tiny blue Honda, in exchange for not losing Laurie's friendship.

A trade. There were balances in the Universe. You never got anything for nothing.

Nick called again, his voice splintered and breaking. Jill didn't respond. She threw the phone against the wall, cut off Laurie's voice and sprinted for the stairs.

Nick was on his hands and knees in the bedroom, his head hanging. His body shuddered as he coughed, a thick and heavy sound. He tried to raise his head toward her. She grabbed him, pulled him to his feet, Nick flailing and fighting her. His hands fisted at chest level.

She had no idea how to stop it.

"Call 9-1-1." Agony grayed his face and he tried to slide back down. She eased him to the floor, grabbed the phone beside the bed and called for an ambulance. Her heart raced. Time stood still. When she turned to him again Nick's arms were covered in blood.

Jill stopped moving. Her mind raced. "Did you cut yourself?"

Stupid question. How could he answer? He was in so much pain– but his voice was a little stronger, a little less hoarse. "It's – yours."

"Mine?" But her hands were slick with it. Her fingers burned from razor cuts. She stared, appalled. The blood on the vellum sheets. The slick wet red ink. The dried red brown writing in the grimoire. "I don't under–"

"Yes, you *do*." His voice stronger again and then her cell rang, battered and cracked but ringing from the landing and Nick fell again, sliding hard to the floor.

"You have to undo whatever you did."

Her fingers started to bleed heavily, the bedroom carpet turning red where she stood. Jill looked between Nick and her hands.

"*Jill.*"

She looked at him. The phone rang in her hand and she ignored it.

Could be paramedics with an ETA or asking directions. She didn't think it mattered. Nick was going to be all right or not depending on her.

Nick took a very careful breath, as if trying not to startle any pain to life, and said, "Whatever you did, you have to undo it."

The grimoire, and Laurie. She'd made a trade. She'd seen it in portal after portal, world after world. Every action had an equal and opposite reaction. Everything had a price. All these years she'd missed Laurie so much she'd carried a lost college friendship into her 30s. In danger of losing a friendship now to one lost in a past she couldn't let go of.

For a lost friend so selfish she had almost killed them both.

"I don't know what to do." Her voice trembled, panic returning, but Nick sat up on his own, one hand braced against the floor, the other reaching for hers. She took it and held on and her lacerated fingers throbbed against his sweat-slick skin.

"Take back whatever you did. It's in that book. The grimoire you bought."

She nodded, and argued at the same time. "How will I find–"

"You don't have to," Nick said. "Did you look at the back of the book when you bought it? In the second half of the book? Really look at it?"

When she shook her head he went on.

"It's a book of halves. The first is written – it exists. Angels, demons, I don't know. You said –" He panted for breath, shook his head when she started to panic and reach for the phone – "You saw angelic script or what the book said was."

Her hand paused. She didn't touch the phone. "Yes?"

"The first half of the book."

She shook her head. "All of it."

And he shook his head back at her. "The first half of the book, Jill. The rest of it is blank."

Laurie. She'd wanted Laurie back, the guilt gone, to have everything she'd had. And the wet red ink on the pages. The cuts on her fingertips. All the worlds, everything she'd seen – all of it hers. Her life. Her story. But that made sense. What didn't — "I don't know Latin," she said.

Nick sat on the floor now, one hand still against his chest, but more like he had a cold, or asthma. "It's not in Latin."

From outside she could just hear the sirens. "I don't know magic."

Nick almost smiled. Almost shrugged. But the pain was still there. "The book does."

When she looked at him, he said, "You don't know how an airplane works but you know how to ride one to where you want to go."

Jill stood, letting go of Nick's hand.

"I have to send Laurie back."

"God, yes."

Relief on his face for just an instant and then he folded, nearly in half, and from the landing her cell began to scream, first ringing, then Laurie's voice: *You bitch, you whore, you can't leave me here – your fault – he doesn't love you, I was your best friend –*

But Jill was running, out of the bedroom, halfway down the stairs, past the shattered, shrieking cell, to her alcove, the big window where the moonlight still came through, amazing everything had happened so fast when it seemed to take so long. Upstairs she could hear Nick starting to cough again and she pleaded, with him, with herself, *hold on, only a couple minutes, hold on* – because the sirens were forever away and in her heart she knew she could save him.

She could.

The grimoire burned. She ignored the pain, dragged it onto her lap, turned to a blank page and started writing, one fingernail digging the words in, engraving them almost, the bloody tip of her finger smearing blood into the lines she opened in time and space. She didn't know how to fix this, did she open a portal and push them through to next week? Next month? Avoid whatever happened in between? But what if something went wrong? What if she only came out a week or a month or a day later without Nick?

Backward, then. And she reversed her writing, unwrote the days, the lawn mowing, the burning breakfast, the bookstore, all of it like a rewound videotape, like a DVD scanning backward through scenes, swirling backward in jerky movements, her and Nick – and Nick – and Nick.

The book dropped out of her hands. She reached for it but it was no longer on the floor at her feet. She fell to her knees, searching wildly, hands and eyes. Nothing but darkness, as if the lights had gone out and the moon gone away and everything gone and left her alone.

From the bedroom, Nick's voice, thick with sleep: "Jill?"

She ran. Tripped on the bottom stair and almost sent herself flying. Up past the library loft, up and up and the bedroom never this far before. Into the bedroom, squinting because the bedside light on Nick's side seemed blinding.

He was up on one elbow in bed, covers mostly turned back in the September chill, as if he'd been about to get up and come after her. He relaxed visibly when he saw her. "Couldn't sleep?"

Terror and shock and loss slammed into her. She couldn't speak. Her eyes filled with tears and she took a step closer to the bed.

The pounding started downstairs on the front door and she realized she'd heard sirens winding off.

"What's that?" He shoved the covers off altogether and pulled on his robe, the two of them heading downstairs together, turning the porch light on and confronting the young patrolman on the doorstep. He squinted into the light.

"I'm sorry to wake you. There's been an accident on your street." And past him they could see Nick's truck on the street, the back mangled out of recognition and the tiny blue Honda, nearly half of it under the truck, as if the driver had headed straight for Nick's truck, never braking. Never slowing. The EMTs were loading a stretcher into the back of the ambulance. A stretcher with a body bag.

"I'm sorry. We think the driver might have been headed here," the patrolman said as they stepped out onto the welcome mat. "Registration said the car belonged to a Laurie Taylor. Do you–"

But the look on Jill's face made him stop. "Ma'am, I'm very sorry for your loss."

Jill nodded. "Thank you." Even to herself her voice sounded like she was asleep, or very far away. In another world. "She's someone I knew a very long time ago. I haven't seen her in years." She stepped back toward the house and took Nick's hand tight in hers.

"Did you know she was coming to see you?" the cop asked.

"I'm not sure she was," Jill said. "I think maybe she was going somewhere else entirely." Nick's hand tightened on hers and she knew he'd have a million questions. She'd told him Laurie was dead, mourned that friendship for the last 15 years or so.

Nick himself had explained the grimoire to her, so he should understand, but the grimoire was gone, tucked back into last week where it couldn't touch them, her fingertips healed, time reversed.

Worlds on top of worlds. Like a stack of transparent playing cards set on end.

In one of those worlds, Nick would believe her. If she could just find it.

The book could lead her. The book, at the bookstore. Waiting. Surely no one would have bought it in the last week. She was sure she could find it. She could almost hear it calling to her.

This time, she knew what to do.

In the summer of 2012, my husband and I were starting to think we'd never find a house we liked and get out of the tiny town we'd moved to and back into Reno. Then our fabulous realtor found us our house in Reno's rural North Valleys, with lots of land and foothills for a back yard. We bid, won the bid and then, for too many reasons to explain, lost the house.

Frustrated and cranky and thinking we were never going to find what we wanted, I wrote a story in which I thoroughly haunted the North Valleys house – following which, we got the house after all.

... I never turn my back on the upstairs window when I'm in the garden.

Housewarming

The new house held on to the violence from the previous owners.

If Tim sensed it, Jenna had no proof. He saw the results, of course. There was no way to miss the results. But he didn't *feel* it.

He'd be grateful for that if he knew, she thought, and crossed the once-blue, now-sodden-gray carpet to take the few steps across the "dining area" and look out the back door. The house was smaller than what they owned in a tiny desert town an hour away. The move would put them back into an actual city, albeit on the outskirts. That wasn't so bad, really. The outskirts meant she'd already seen an squirrel and a blue bellied lizard in their soon-to-be back yard and the view from the dented, tired stainless steel kitchen sink was of the Sierra. The neighborhood was quiet, without the constant dogs and neighbors at their current house, and the new house sat on a third of an acre rather than the postage stamp lot they currently occupied where even though it was a single family house, the could sometimes hear people next door sneeze.

But the violence.

"They took out all the light fixtures," Tim said. He sounded a little bewildered. True, light fixtures were a weird choice, but the blue-taped notice in the front window meant the family there before them – with children whose bathroom was decorated in fish stickers – had been foreclosed and evicted.

Jenna thought she might rip off light fixtures and take the microwave if she was in their shoes.

What she wouldn't have done was the waist-level holes clearly punched into walls and doors, the holes that went straight through walls into other rooms in some cases, and upstairs in one of the two bedrooms they'd pulled up the carpet and taken the carpet padding, as well as removing the closet doors and gluing something sticky to the shelves in the closet.

The missing carpet bothered her. The house bothered her, the way it never seemed to rest. As if someone had just exited whatever room they walked into. The violence swarmed like a black thundercloud about three feet above the floor.

In the summer heat of the closed upstairs, Jenna shivered.

"Hey," Tim called unexpectedly from downstairs. "There's a swimming pool."

"It doesn't show in the pictures of the back yard," she said when she'd joined him. The back yard was spacious, ringed in evergreens which her virulent allergies insisted would be ripped up and disposed of, replaced with apple trees and wild flowers. Just below the spot where the sides of the yard sloped up, the way the street sloped up toward foothill, a small shed squatted on blocks, looking like Baba Yaga's chicken-footed residence. Tim had speculated the owners had avoided taxes on the structure by not having a foundation. Jenna had speculated the shed got up and ran around during the full moon, maybe snapping up neighbors for sustenance.

"Did that happen in the Baba Yaga tales?" Tim asked.

She shrugged. "No clue. Maybe Terry Pratchett."

The real mystery was the padlocked chain that wrapped all the way around the 12x12 structure and ended in a complicated mess of door handle and bolt, chain and padlock and, for no very good reason, a length of light cotton rope that fluttered whitely in the hot desert wind like a thin ghost.

The back yard, like the front, boasted sere desert dirt, though someone had made an attempt at a rose garden just outside the bedroom window.

The thorns were doing better than the flowers.

The house was that way. Standoffish. Thorny. It held them at bay, as if uncomfortable with the idea of anyone occupying its rooms again. The yard itself was pure desert, all dirt and the evergreens and roses struggling in the dry climate.

Behind the house rose a desert foothill, from the top of which Jenna figured she'd be able to see into one of the North Valleys closer to Reno. There were above-ground power lines behind the house. Come winter she'd hear the wind singing in the wires when the storms roared off the mountains.

Now, though, July, hot summer, she stood staring in wonder. The Department of Housing and Urban Development had foreclosed and marketed the house, and someone had come in and taken careful pictures, de-emphasizing the stained and filthy carpet, the torn up linoleum, the holes in the doors and drywall. But the real talent had been shooting snaps of the back yard from every angle and not including the above-ground swimming pool.

"They took the liner out," Tim said, standing with his elbows on the rim of the pool. Neither of them were swimmers. Jenna had a tendency to nearly drown if she even got close to water. Tim just wasn't interested.

"They left the filter," Jenna said. "And a net."

"You could plant tomatoes in there," he said, peering in. The inside of the pool had filled in with desert sand.

"Or use it as the world's biggest cat box," she said.

"You clean it, then," he said, and turned to look up at the window that lit the landing at the top of the stairs. From inside there was a tremendous view of the mountains.

From outside the window was dark. Jenna turned away as Tim aimed the camera up. He wanted to document every step of the transformation from HUD house to Their house. She was staring critically at the evergreens when she felt him tense beside her, going completely still.

His voice was soft. "Did we leave the front door unlocked?"

She hadn't looked up yet, hadn't looked away from the greenery. The yard simmered around them, clear sky and hot sun heating the dirt. "Of course so," she said. The realtor's lock box was broken and the house was in escrow and they all were leaving the key under a rock in the front yard. Probably highly unorthodox for real estate agents, but theirs was a flighty female who was convinced they weren't supposed to even enter the house until every I was dotted and T crossed. Since the government owned the house, it was possible she was right.

"Someone?" Tim said, and it came out a question Jenna really didn't like.

He touched her then, his hand like ice on her upper arm, and she didn't want to look at him so she looked up to the window at the landing.

The stark white face with sunken black eyes screamed. Blood splashed from the lips.

From where they stood in the yard, they could hear no sound at all.

Time stretched out. It felt like hours passed while they stood staring at the face.

If it looks at us, I'll scream, Jenna thought. The thing in the window stared up and out, maybe at the distant mountains.

Maybe at nothing.

"Come on." Tim's voice. Shaky but sure. That was their house. There was someone in it. There shouldn't be.

She couldn't tell if he was seeing the same thing she was. She didn't ask. She followed him, a close jog, almost on his heels as he crossed the yard and hit the back door that led into the master bedroom. The face was in the window in the instant before she barreled into the bedroom. No time for anyone to have come down the stairs – they'd hear them, encounter them in the short hall between bedroom and stairs.

She smacked into Tim where he'd stopped at the foot of the stairs. There was no one on the landing.

From the edge of the hallway they could see both the tiny efficiency kitchen and the dining space, the closed and locked glass sliding door to the side yard, the living room with its devastated carpet. The front door, closed.

"Upstairs," Tim said quietly. If someone was up there, no point pretending they weren't coming. As soon as they started up the 10 thickly carpeted steps she could see not only was the landing empty but that the window was still closed. That left two bedrooms, two closets, both of which the doors had been removed from, one hall closet built over the stairs and the bathroom where there were no shower doors, no shower curtain. They'd see in instants if the house was empty.

She didn't want to see that.

The upstairs was empty. By unspoken agreement and 12 years of marriage, Jenna stayed in the hall to watch for anyone coming out of the bedrooms Tim wasn't in. She didn't like standing outside the first bedroom

- it was too close to the landing. When she looked out the window at the edge of the yard she could see without being *on* the landing or too close to the window, she imagined she could see the face, reflected somehow, though really standing where she was she'd see the back of the head.

If there was a back of head to see.

"Stop it," she said aloud and Tim was back out with her, having ducked into the first room only to look into closet, behind door and test the window.

"What did you say?"

"Imagination," she said.

If he understood, he didn't say. He passed her, went into the second bedroom, the one she meant to take for her office, the one where the carpet had been ripped up. She heard him make a sound of disgust and she went promptly to join him. It only took a second to open the door to the closet over the stairs and poke her head into the bathroom. She already knew she'd find no one.

"What did you say?" she asked him.

She didn't need to. The room reeked. There hadn't been a smell like this before. The house did smell, of the years of cigarette smoke that had yellowed the walls throughout, of neglect and the kind of ozone smell of the type of anger that leaves holes in the drywall.

This wasn't that. This wasn't even the downstairs carpet which had been drenched twice in as many weeks as Tim tested the water throughout the house. It worked. What didn't work were the pipes under the bathroom sink, sabotaged by the previous owners to blow the minute they were turned on. Water had started to pool under the sink, then gathered energy and poured out, running to the edges of the bathroom, all the connecting places where room met room, where lino met carpet, where joists met and structural walls mattered. It ran into the HVAC ducting that honeycombs all houses and poured through the cold air return, unattractively located at the edge of the living room. By the time they'd gotten downstairs, there was a full scale thunderstorm pouring water onto the once-blue carpet.

This wasn't that. This was the stench of – "Garbage?" Tim asked.

Jenna had always had a more sensitive sense of smell. She smelled skunk before he did, or smoke, or natural gas. It played into all those stereotypes of the nervous female asking, "Honey, do you smell smoke?" but she was usually right.

"Blood," Jenna said, and looked again at the bare plywood floor where the carpet had been carried way.

She stepped back hurriedly out of the room, standing in the hall with her hands on the banister above the staircase, and looked without thinking toward the landing window. From this far back in the house she could see into the back yard.

Without intending to, she stared at the shed.

"I don't know what to tell you," Regina, their realtor, said for the third time. Tim had called her and had to repeat himself to get through to her, his voice rising in a way Jenna hadn't heard in a while. Regina was freaked because Jenna and Tim were not supposed to be in the house unless they were meeting a realtor, either the listing agent who talked faster than a meth head on a high, or Regina herself, who had a thick accent and an attitude so positive it bordered on mania and often had no basis in reality. It was all right for them to lay out cash for earnest money and again when the loan dudes failed to file on time and escrow was extended, but heaven forbid the buyers go in the house alone.

Only they weren't sure they had been alone. That was the point. And Jenna was very unhappy hearing Tim's voice rise as he got louder and louder, finally shouting if Regina would shut the hell up and listen for god's sake he could explain that whoever had been in the house wasn't them. And the house had been closed up and yes, they were in the back yard and the front door unlocked, but there was no way anyone got past them.

And on the third run through, Jenna took the phone from him, her hand only shaking a little. Things had been better between them. For years. No need to worry that his fury was going to wake just because –

Just because it was? She asked herself.

Or just because this house is full of it? Of rage, of anger that floats like something I can see. The way I used to see it springing off of Tim like energy, like a black aura. She told Regina the basics - that all they'd wanted to relay was that someone had been in the house, and what did the realtor want to do about it, if anything?

The house was perfect in so many ways. Location (location, location, the way realtors said it three times like it was a mantra), the foothills and the crows, the big back yard and the lack of neighbors and that was all right now, she didn't have to be surrounded by impatient acquaintances who would call the police.

Because there had been help for both of them, one on one therapy and anger management, all those groups and only one fist fight during them.

They'd gotten through all of it and the house was their reward. The house fit the bill for them. It got them back into the northern suburbs of Reno rather than the exile they'd felt 35 miles east in the tiny desert town of Nothing Much. It was close to their work. It was less expensive. It would give them projects to work on together as they remodeled (never mind the horror stories she had heard from friends about remodeling and the therapy required afterwards, some of it liquid therapy). It had to be that Tim's anger was only spilling over because the realtor was being flighty and dense and hung up on the "Don't ever go in alone" thing. Jenna was willing to bet the entire reason for that was to cover the realtor in case something happened. In case someone did stumble into the home where Regina insisted Tim and Jenna couldn't be.

OK. That was it. Tim's anger was situational. Understandable. It was not caused by some kind of free floating fury leftover in the house, something attracted to Tim because of his past angers.

And the face?

She shuddered, and rubbed her arms, and listened to a calmer Tim who had the phone again and was agreeing to call a locksmith and wait while both locksmith and management company taking care of the house for the duration of escrow arrived.

"So what do you think the face was?" Jenna asked as summer dusk sent up the scents of sage and dirt. The truck was hot, the windows down, Tim accelerating as they took the broad highway that led to interstates and back to their current house. Tendrils of Jenna's blond ponytail stuck to her face and neck.

Tim frowned, both hands on the wheel as if he needed to concentrate. There was almost no traffic. "Sunlight hitting the window?"

"Glare?" She didn't consider before she spoke. When she glanced at him his lips had thinned and tightened. Not good. Damn it, the idea that anger was just floating around, waiting to latch on to something – or someone – that was crazy. That was imagination.

She knew it as soon as they got any distance from the house.

The distance between the truck and the house grew and his hands on the wheel relaxed, his right hand letting go, finding hers and holding it. "Did we even see the same thing?"

"How would we know?" They could stop, write down their separate experiences. Nothing in her wanted to do that.

He glanced at her, signaled, and turned onto the highway. "I'll tell you one thing, you tell me, etc."

Fine. "Face."

"White."

"Screaming."

"You heard it?"

That wasn't a description, but he was right.   "Mouth wide open.
Looked like a scream. No, I didn't hear anything."

"I didn't hear anything. Blood."

"From mouth."

"Female."

"White. Very."

"Black eyes," he said.

"Staring. Past us. At – " No idea.

"The hills?" he hazarded, in a voice that thoroughly didn't expect
agreement.

"The shed," Jenna said.

She expected to have nightmares that night. She wasn't wrong.

Buying a HUD house wasn't like buying their first house, the exile in
Fernley house, had been. That had been straightforward even if it had been
a long process. They'd picked out the model of the house and the lot while
a subdivision was building up during the housing insanity in 2004. They'd
waited as the bubble started bursting around them and the neighborhood
built up and their house was finally ready, through delays caused by broken
trusses the developer hoped they wouldn't notice and sliding glass doors put
in the wrong place, thermometers installed in bathroom walls and one closet
the builders tried to turn into a bathroom. Eventually they signed papers
with a crazy cat title lady who pointed out where to sign here, here and here
with very long French manicure. In June, when they moved in, the Nevada
weather celebrated by snowing until the last box was unloaded.

The HUD house was different. It was federal government, for one
thing, which meant none of the procedures made sense and despite the fact
that the neighborhood and the house had both been standing for more than
16 years, it looked likely the process would take longer than that to get them
moved in.

And the realtor, rightly or wrongly, continued to insist they stay away
unless there were inspections to be made or utilities to be turned on or
unless she was with them. Jenna thought Regina, who became more and
more wound up and insanely positive and delighted, would likely adopt

whatever they'd seen in the window and drive it away with the sheer force and volume of her Cheerful Chatter.

She thought that when they were arranging meetings or signing papers or producing endless streams of financial data. When she was at the house, approved or trespassing, she didn't feel flippant. She felt nervous. Oppressed.

Scared.

And hopeful. She loved the mountains, the desert, the blue belly lizard in the back yard. The swish and sway of traffic on the side street, the call of crows over the foothills.

The lure of the shed in the back.

Tim found her there, staring at the lock. They'd come to tack down very cheap carpet from a home improvement store to make the county inspector happy. He didn't care what it was – the probably could have covered the floor with rag rugs from a dollar store or cast-off t-shirts – just that federal regs said they couldn't move in with bare plywood and they didn't have the money yet for real carpet. The entire time Tim had been in that room, nailing down cheap indoor-outdoor flat gray carpet cut with a utility knife and already unraveling at the edges, she'd been tense, pacing downstairs with nothing much to do. She'd kept trying to go into the room where he was, unconsciously batting at the coils of black cloud that seemed thick that day, and finally Tim had shouted at her, told her to get out, for the love of god, and let him work.

She'd recoiled. For an instant the face bellowing hadn't been Tim's angular, almost feline face. She'd seen in place of his straight dark hair and blue eyes a wider, coarser face, red-brown shaggy hair, a nose that had been broken. Just for an instant. And her crazy heart had soared, because it wasn't Tim shouting at her. Not Tim returning to the past years of anger, that core of fury from an abusive childhood and the fear of chasing his own dreams.

Then she'd bolted anyway. Tim wasn't the only one with demons from the past to overcome. Whatever was yelling, it needed time to calm down. The ozone stench needed to fade. And the trembling fear inside her needed to back down.

At the landing she'd all but plunged down the 10 stairs. She'd missed the first of the three steps up, turned an ankle and caught the scarred and flaking metal banister that rocked precariously in her fevered grip, and almost fell. She caught herself, the leg on the outside of her pivot point already circling around and over and down to the next stair down the long side of the flight. She let it, her hand sliding sweat-slick along the metal and her other hand finding the metal hand rail. She hit the stair tread hard, her teeth clicking together, and then she was just heading downstairs, a controlled free fall, her heart pounding in fear.

A hard left, through the short hall, away from the stairs, the landing where the face had been, the upstairs were Tim was. Through the bedroom, the back door already open, and into the sunlight that felt as life-affirming as taking a breath.

She stopped then, and looked up into the landing window. She couldn't have stopped herself if she'd tried.

The face was there, screaming. Dark hair, white, white face. Blood red mouth because there was blood. Sunken eyes.

Please don't be looking at me.

The eyes were trained on the shed.

Tim found Jenna standing in front of the shed. The late afternoon desert sunlight was growing long. She saw his shadow before she heard his footsteps on the barren dirt. A cringe tried to work through her muscles and she forced it down, the same way she'd forced herself to turn her back on the upstairs window and study the door to the shed.

He hasn't been angry in years. It's not like it was. This is a stupid system of home buying. He's just frustrated. So are you.

Good pep talk. She was actually afraid, though. Of the house. Of Tim. Of the house *and* Tim.

She turned anyway and tried to smile at her own foolishness. Only Tim wasn't smiling. He carried a toolbox which he handed her and when she held it out, feeling slightly like a scrub nurse, he opened it and removed the tools he needed and quickly, dexterously, removed the hex bolts holding the door closed.

She held her breath and thought that Tim did, too. The wide door swung open, letting out a rush of stale, hot air.

The inside of the shed was empty but the floor boards were stained, scuffed and laid down unevenly, a few bent upward. The air inside reeked of old pennies, fear, ozone and despair.

Jenna thought she could feel the woman from the upstairs window reach forward to touch the back of her neck, exposed where a ponytail held her hair out of her way. Ice coursed through her veins and she sidestepped quickly, out of reach of nothing there, nothing behind her, only an empty shed and Tim, beside her, looking furious again though not, she thought, at her.

Neither of them turned to look at the house or the window behind them. Jenna pulled her cell from the back pocket of her shorts and called the police.

Turned out to be county sheriff's office that responded where the new house was located. A laconic American West sheriff's deputy with broad shoulders and a permanent squint answered the call.

"This is going to play hell with your escrow," he said, and moved a toothpick from one side of his mouth to the other.

Neither of them could think of anything to say to that so they just showed him the way in to the house and through to the back yard because the gates were still padlocked even though half the time when they'd been looking at the house before they made a bid the house itself had been unlocked.

The sheriff's deputy stopped on the front porch and nodded. "I was out here once. Happened too often, the calls that got logged."

Jenna met Tim's eyes. He raised his brows and shrugged. The cop saw the interchange in the glass slider before they exited into the back yard. Jenna went ahead anyway.

"Can you tell us anything?"

Sheriff shrugged. "Public record, really. First couple times we came out we figured he was a D&D."

Dungeons and dragons? Jenna wondered. "What?"

"Drunk and disorderly. But he wasn't." He paused on the brick patio just outside the bedroom where a tree stood much too close to the house, full of orange berries and hope but with roots threatening the foundations and Tim threatening the tree's continued existence. "He was far from disorderly. He was kind of pathological and organized and bone mean and probably crazy." He nodded back at the house. "Mad, too. You've noticed the holes." It wasn't a question.

"Hard to miss," Tim said, and then they all moved to the shed.

"We'll have to call forensics," he said, looking into the shed. He sniffed, tentatively, and nodded. "I'm sorry it will delay your escrow."

"This is more important," Jenna said, and saw Tim's hands fisted by his sides. Oh, very much more important, both for the living and the dead. And the thought shook her and she looked up at the house, but the window was empty.

*****

For a surprise, they weren't sent away when the investigative unit arrived. They were asked to stay and Jenna tried sitting in the truck, but the day was too hot and when Regina joined them, along with the listing agent, which was only to be expected, Jenna supposed, the three of them went inside, standing in the kitchen, making the sort of desultory conversation that people make when stuck in slow-moving emergencies with people they have nothing in common with.

Tim went outside, answering questions Jenna would later have to answer, standing a good distance away from the shed, Jenna saw from the bedroom before she went back to the kitchen.

Regina couldn't think of anything positive about the situation.

"Did anyone know them?" Jenna asked finally, because no one was saying anything and she couldn't stop wondering what might be standing at the top of the stairs. If she moved just a few feet from kitchen to dining area, she'd be able to see most of the way up the stairs and she didn't want to.

"Doesn't usually work that way," the listing agent, Kathy, said. "It's repossessed by the bank, becomes real estate owned, goes on the market through whatever agency thinks it can sell it."

"But?" Jenna prompted. Because Kathy had said "doesn't usually" not "that's not how it works." As in *ever*.

Kathy shrugged, and pulled it off badly. "They were angry. Foreclosed, evicted, given 30 days to clear out. We came in at 40 days and they were still here."

"No one checked?" Realtors were often women. She'd assumed the sheriff's office would check things out before anyone went in.

"Market's picking up," Regina said. "Inventory of new homes is going down. Existing homes are starting to sell. No one took the time."

Kathy didn't shrug this time. "He was one mean SOB."

Regina nodded. "And she was the B."

"What?" The house was summer hot. No one had opened any windows, not quite admitting they didn't want to hear what was going on in the back yard. There was no air conditioning. But a shiver of cold went down the back of Jenna's neck in the heat.

"Oh, yeah," Kathy said. "Piece of work. She made him look sweet."

Big man, reddish hair, nose that had been broken. That air of fury, the ozone black stench of rage Jenna had smelled for so many years as their funds dwindled and the bubble broke and they got stuck in a house they loved in a town they hated, 40 miles away from rapidly distancing friends. The fights, the therapy, the groups.

The reconciliations. Not everybody got those.

"Where'd they go?" Jenna asked, and when Kathy cocked her head at the question, "I mean, did they – " leave a forwarding in case anyone wanted to send them more bills and demands? "Did they leave a forwarding address?" She thought Kathy was crazy and Regina a twit. Why shouldn't she ask?

"Original thought was they went out of state. Dropped out of sight of creditors, probably staying with relatives and not the ones listed on the paperwork when they bought the place." Kathy had started to pace, her thick rubber wedge flip flops making Jenna's calves ache sympathetically.

What did the wife look like? How was she supposed to ask that? *I think I've seen her, screaming in my window. But then, I think the sheriff's deputies will find her pretty quick.* And then again, these weren't women she wanted to keep as friends once the eternal, unending process of buying the house ended.

"What did she look like?"

Kathy had paced outside, frightening the lizard away as she stepped out the slider on the kitchen side of the house, the far side from where the shed was being tested, or whatever was going on. Regina, distracted by a text, manicure flying, said, "Pretty but harsh. Smoker's mouth. Long dark hair."

Blue eyes. Right? Blue eyes that sometimes looked black?

"Really dark blue eyes."

She almost went out then, but the censoring looks she figured the investigative team would give her stopped her, that and Tim would be there, and she wasn't quite ready to see him yet. Fear pulsed inside her chest.

From outside the bedroom slider she heard someone shout, and others join him, and then she heard a wrenching, grating sound, followed by multiple male voices shouting. Her hands balled into fists. She walked out of the kitchen, Regina still saying something, her positive on again. Down the three-step hall, through the master bedroom of decaying carpet and late day sunlight coming from the back yard.

The shed had tipped coming off its foundation, probably causing the first of the group shouts.

The crime scene unit was only two deputies, plus the original and Tim meant four guys standing back from the shed as if they expected it to rock up onto those stone pillar-y feet and come after them. The shed lay three-quarters of the way onto its back, kind of toppled turtle pose. Jenna slid past Tim and stared.

There was a hand coming up from the hole dug, she assumed, about the place where the scuffed, broken floorboard had been. She doubted anyone in the back yard was surprised by this.

The fact that the hand belonged to a male probably surprised everyone but Jenna.

"She must have dragged him through the back yard, loosened the floorboards, dug down underneath the shed."

The forensic investigator, who looked about 12, Jenna thought, actually sounded impressed. She didn't know if he was supposed to be telling them anything but then again, they'd all been there and seen the hand and out of all of four of them who weren't law enforcement, Tim might be the only one to not have figured out what almost undoubtedly had happened because he didn't have the insights from the two realtors, or all the thoughts from Jenna's head.

Then again, maybe he understood perfectly the moment the shed was moved and the first layer of dirt shoveled off.

"She must be a huge woman," the investigator said, closing up his tablet with a scrunch of his fingers and blinking away from the dirt and at the circle of women. "I mean," he blushed. "If that's what – "

"Probably," Kathy said. She seemed unable to look away from the body. Now they were all waiting on a coroner's van while plastic numbers like those placed on restaurant tables so waitresses could deliver orders were placed in the dirt around the vacated shed.

"I mean," the investigator said, flushing further.

"No," Jenna said, feeling the anger rise. "She wasn't big." She didn't care if the realtors stared at her, and actually they didn't seem to be looking at her at all. "She was thin, not wiry but just thin, tall and not very strong."

The realtors were staring up at the window above the landing. They seemed frozen, unable to look away.

Jenna didn't follow their gaze. She just looked at the investigator and said, "It's amazing what rage will do. How much stronger it makes you."

Jenna knew. The rush of strength probably came from the same place adrenaline surges came from, the ones that allowed ordinary wives to pick cars off of husbands. Tim's anger had caused blowups and shouting matches, long nights where neither could sleep and neither would back down.

But it was Jenna's anger that led to phone books torn in half and one entire stack of dishes lifted at once and thrown. Jenna's anger, leftover from *her* childhood, that burned as bright as Tim's.

The men had gone back to the hand sticking up from the floor of the shed, the floor that remained in place as if the shed itself was a camper shell resting on the foundation and floor. Jenna looked down slowly and saw her hands had tightened to fists.

The anger and violence leftover in the house had wakened Jenna's anger, not Tim's. She'd heard him raise his voice and cringed in case it was anger and in case that anger came at her. But Tim's frustration was under control.

She wasn't sure about her own.

If she looked up at the window over the landing now, she thought the face there would have green eyes and blond hair pulled back in a ponytail.

The police would handle what had happened here, which was all too obvious. Even if it turned out to be a different story than what it appeared, Jenna thought it would still be the same in spirit.

Let law enforcement do its thing. It was time for Jenna and Tim to do theirs. She didn't turn toward the window, but moved across the dry desert dirt of the back yard to where Tim stood and forced her hands to relax so that she could slide one of hers into his.

It was time for them to change the spirit of the house.

In the Shape of a Heart

The bodega stood in the middle of nowhere, dark wood against the white sands of the desert. It stood just off the two lane highway that ran from the middle of nowhere where we lived to the next spot over. The small wood building nestled up against the edge of the hills and Denise pointed it out at once. That made sense; she was always the type to want to stop and look. It was only a few miles from home but I didn't come this way often and had never seen it before and besides, Vincent wasn't due home for a couple hours yet, so I signaled for any potential traffic and turned off the highway into the gravel filled parking lot.

Two steps led up to the recessed front door – more like a private residence than a shop – and we stepped through into the smell of burning herbs and a lack of sunlight. It was early April but the sun was beating down with August fury. The heat felt good on my sore muscles, on assorted bruises, but the direct sunlight was dizzying.

The woman behind the counter looked us over as we stepped in. she looked almost like my grandmother, or like I expected I would look in 30 years. Her hair was white as the sand outside and she wore thick black rimmed glasses. I thought perhaps she was reading our auras, checking out our souls and discerning our intentions. But just as likely she expected us to be tourist types, there to laugh and giggle in undertones while pretending belief or at least reverence for someone else's.

It seemed an odd place for a bodega, between suburbs, kind of nowhere, but living at the southern edge of Arizona there were few who hadn't played at some kind of magic or another. Indian, often, pirated and encrypted beyond recognition. As close to the border as we were it could well be Mexican magic, prostituted into some unrecognizable form, made cheap, easy and attainable by the masses. Instant magic, not the traditional like the magic that passed down through Vincent's family.

I tried to imagine it as a real place, tried to imagine the dark skinned women coming in wearing shapeless dresses, dark eyes smoldering as they bought candles and oils and herbs. Or young men, coming in to buy black candles and red ribbons, binding the girls close to them, girls they'd leave the moment a hint of fat or age showed on slim, young bodies.

I glanced at the clock behind the counter, something like an overgrown pocket watch, the numerals Roman and the hands spinning quickly. Time marched forward to quickly anymore, always dangerously fast, dangerously close to time for me to be home and attentive and behaved. There was never time anymore for even the most temporary escapes.

Denise had moved away from me when I looked at the clock, stepped between two tables and broke a string that stretched there. It wasn't the first; the place was strung with them like a web. I looked around for Denise.

She was across the room from me, holding up a carved rock, a small stone the size of the palm of her hand, intricately carved in the shape of a heart and bound with a red ribbon.

"Angie, look," she said, dangling the thing. "Do you think it's a charm?" It looked a little like something Vincent had given me back before everything changed.

"I think it's beautiful," I said, taking it gently in my own hands. I expected the cool of rock but the thing was hot and moist and when I took it, it gave a little jolt, as if attempting to beat, and I dropped it hurriedly back on the table and stepped away.

Across from me, where Denise had stood, now was a man. I nodded at him but his eyes didn't vary; he just stared. Between his fingers he stretched a length of the threads that bound this place, the ends coiled around his fingers as if he held a garrote. I felt a sudden thrill of fear. His eyes looked wrong, shattered somehow, or faceted. Like Vincent's, eyes that seemed to follow me wherever I turned, everywhere I went, as if there were no leaving him behind.

I looked around for Denise but she was across the store, heading for a wall of books. When I looked back at the man, he stood directly in front of me.

"Get away from me," I said. I could break the thread with one finger – I'd already broken several. But I needed to speak. Assert myself. He stepped back, muttered "Excuse me," as if I were simply an intemperate shopper, moved away without speaking again but I could still feel his gaze. Even the way he moved was strange, as if he were used to moving faster, hovering lower. His upper body leaned out, straining to be horizontal to the floor; his arms reached forward as if they helped him walk.

I squinted across the store, looking for Denise. The little shop was dark, not like the sun had gone behind clouds but like night had fallen. My heart pounded at the thought it might be later than I had expected, but it was still afternoon and Vincent wasn't expected home until this evening. "I'm going to call home and see if there are any messages," I told Denise, pulling my phone from my purse. With things so tense between Vincent and me, I wasn't going to take a chance of being late. I wasn't going to take any chances at all.

"Sure," she said and tried not to let me see the sympathy in her dark eyes before she turned back to the wall of books. I went out to the front step and sat on the edge of it, fiddling with the phone until it made sense to me again. The phone was new. One more gift from Vincent. One more way for him to track me. He always knew where I was anyway.

The phone at home rang four times before the machine picked up and I waited to hear my own vaguely uncertain voice telling me I wasn't home but instead Vincent's voice came on, hot and harsh.

"It would all work out much better if you would just stay home like you're supposed to," Vincent said. "Forever."

I turned cold beneath the battering sunlight. He meant to kill me. This time. This time he wouldn't stop. Forever, he'd said. Vincent, whose beliefs included that only death was forever.

"Will you love me forever?" I'd asked when we were young and in love and his intensity thrilled me. I wanted to be possessed by a man who loved me so much he was jealous of everyone around me. Will you love me forever? "Only death is forever," he told me but he gave me the necklace then, something destroyed at some later time, a thin golden shimmer of heart threaded through by chain.

Symbolic, now.

I thrust the phone back into my purse, then remembered to fumble after it and turn it off. The bodega seemed cooler than before and the incense more cloying. The look on my face was enough to tell Denise something was wrong. I turned to drag her toward the exit but the man with the shattered eyes blocked my path, so like Vincent in those moments before the violence started.

Instant jolting revulsion. He looked like Vincent, who couldn't know where I was (always knows where I am. Always will.) My hand flew to my face – sore cheekbones, sore mouth – just as quickly struck out to push him away, sure that now a totally different stranger would be standing there when I blinked. Someone offended or curious or afraid. Someone blond and pale to Vincent's dark. Someone so unlike my husband as to be unimaginable.

The dark man reached out. He was older than Vincent, puffy with alcohol or lack of sleep, bristling with dark hair along his arms. Suddenly he looked nothing at all like my husband. "Are you all right? I didn't mean to startle – "

"Don't *touch* me!" Backing away, and I felt Denise's hand on my shoulder.

"C'mon, hon, it's so hot today. Let's go get an iced tea."

I tried to nod, tried to keep my eyes on the dark man as I tried to back out of the store. Something caught at my ankle and I reached down for it. Another of the damned strings. I snapped it but it stuck to my fingers and I shook my hands convulsively, rubbed them against my shorts, and all the while Denise pulled and the man advanced. Something else behind me and I turned, took my eyes off him. The room was thick with strings, passed from point to point, from knickknack to counter top, lamp to floor, so thick they almost held me. I pushed against them, furious, Denise beside me trying to detangle the threads and make a passage and I felt his hands on me, started to turn away and saw the old woman behind the counter. Her hands trailed strings, but she moved them upward, arthritic fingers twining and her mouth moving and the man behind me fell back. His hands came away from my throat, slid from my shoulders, lost purchase on my arms.

I grabbed Denise and ran.

White sunlight. The world disappeared in supernova glare. My hands went to my face. My sunglasses already on and still the white light seared. Denise fumbled at her own sunglasses from the neck of her t-shirt, grabbed my hand because she could see. By the time we made it to the car I could see again through eyes streaming sun tears.

"What's happening?" Denise asked. Arizona streamed past us. I didn't know where I was going. Away. I'd tried a dozen times in the last year, in the last six months, in the last six weeks, to pack a bag, to assemble an escape plan, to put aside some untraceable cash. And every time it fell through. Every time Vincent lovingly scolded me for leaving money laying around. Every time Vincent helped me unpack because I wasn't taking a trip was I let's just put this away sweetheart. I tried to do it and he wasn't home and even then he knew. And then there were repercussions. Corrections. Then things got out of hand.

Other women got pawnable trinkets. I got flowers and verbal apologies. Sometimes he held me especially tight to make sure I understood he was sorry. Sometimes he was so sorry he had to be sorry all over again.

"I have to go," I told Denise. We were heading away from home. "I'll pay your way back." Use the credit cards to get cash, send her back by bus. Disappear. I was crazy. All that time. All that time thinking we could make it work. Nothing's forever, Vincent.

My phone rang. Muffled in my purse, it sounded like a death knell. A glance at the speedometer. We were doing 90. "Could you get that?" I saw her give me a look, then she dug through my purse and grabbed the phone and started to thumb it on.

"Don't answer it!" I returned my eyes to the road, reached for it with one hand.

"Angie," Denise said in Vincent's voice. I arrowed the car toward the side of the road. Denise screamed, herself again, I thought. I tried to think. Slowed to 70 to give myself time to think. Denise was asking me something. I didn't answer. Get to the next town. And get out. Find a bank. Get the largest cash advances possible on my cards. Get Denise home. And get out. Forever. Before forever meant what Vincent wanted it to mean. The next town was 30 miles. We'd –

The car slammed to a stop, rocked as if we'd hit something and the engine raced, the sound of a vehicle stuck in the mud and both of us screamed. I hit the gas and then the brake and nothing made any difference.

"What is it?" Denise slapped the dash. She was half turned in her seat, seat belt throttling her, convinced we were crashing. I forced myself around. I wasn't driving anymore but the car was moving, picking up speed and sailing backward. I managed to turn far enough to see behind us.

Strings. Only a couple of them. But no longer fragile enough to break with one finger.

"What is it?" Denise asked again and I said, "Magic."

The bodega was thick with them. The center of the shop looked like a web gone mad, like an explosion of string with strands running everywhere. The door was blocked open with sticky white. We stood in the entrance and gazed inside. Something in the center of the room scuttled just out of sight. Something with many legs. Something moving very quickly. I started forward.

"You're not going in there?" Denise's hand on my arm. Her eyes were wide in the shadowed shop.

"I have to."

She let go, held on to the door frame as if something inside would suck her in. As if I might ask her to follow. Instead, I said, "Will you wait for me?"

Denise swallowed, and nodded.

Inside the old woman was cocooned, more familiar than ever. Give me 35 years and I'd look just like that. The strings had wound round her, catching arms against her sides, bound up into her hair, immobilizing her. They wrapped around her neck. She saw me and struggled. "You should run" she said and at once several of the strands whipped up and into her mouth, silencing her. Tears ran down her face.

"I can't," is aid. "I'm tired of trying to run." From off to my right by the center of the store I saw movement again, quick and furtive.

Didn't matter. The center was still where I needed to go. The center was where I had seen it, where Denise had held it up on a red ribbon and showed it to me and I didn't know enough to keep hold of it.

I glanced again at the old woman's face as I began pushing my way through the store. Something changed in her expression. She knew what I was looking for. Of course she did.

String so thick I shoved at it with both arms, using my body weight to force strands down and away, twisting over it, under it, between strands, a complicated dance and passage as I forced my way farther in. I could just make out the tables and displays, the goods heaped up and now everything seemed to have bright blue or bright red ribbons tied on, way more red ribbons than I needed, I needed to find one item with a red, red ribbon. Sticky white across the tables, thickening, and the dark man circling, now stalking, now scuttling, now coming closer. I could feel him behind me the way the web shook, by the way the strands around me vibrated. I held my breath. He was close. He could move through this. For him it was not snare but passage. The impulse to look over my shoulder, to see how much he looked like Vincent now, was strong. But I didn't have time. I closed my eyes instead and plunged my hands into the white mass the table had become. A claw brushed my shoulder. Bristly legs grabbed and started to drag me back and up. I yelled, struggled forward and threw myself at the table. The arms lost their grip and there was a sibilant noise, something unworldly, something that should have been inaudible, and webbing shot out, wrapped around my waist and snagged my arms. I grabbed the table and dragged myself forward and away. More strands more legs and a sound like speech, I refused to hear it, knew I'd hear it night after night in my sleep. If I ever slept again. If I ever made it out of here.

I risked a glance at the enormous blackness behind me and beyond it I could just see the old woman. Bound from head to foot she was vanishing into a sticky haze of whiteness.

She was disappearing.

I turned back to the table again just as the legs grabbed me, just as everything started to fall backward and away from me. I grabbed at the table, at the variety of red ribbons. And I had it.

Warm. Thick. It pulsed in my hand, hot, wet. Alive. The white stone breathed life. And silence. As if everything suddenly held its breath.

The stone heart dangled form the red ribbon. Intricately carved, hot and alive. Bound with heart's red ribbon. Talisman. Amulet. Spell stone. I folded it into my hands, breathed Vincent's name into it.

Behind me, something sighed. Fresh air crept into the shop. I kept my eyes closed and between my palms the stone grew hard and smooth and cool. I could feel the markings cut into it. names. Power. Forever, perhaps.

The stone hardened, shrank. My hands came together hard to keep the heart from slipping through my fingers. Light began to seep across my closed eyes, filling the shop. Something dropped away from me with a small soft sound. Strands of webbing brushed my legs, lay across my ankles, and were gone.

I opened my eyes slowly. I held the gold heart-shaped locket in my hands. the thin gold chain wrapped around the red, red ribbon. I looked up into the old woman's eyes. She looked like me. She looked a lot like me. I slipped the necklace over my head. "Can I go home?" I asked.

The woman shrugged. "Do I look like a fortune teller to you?"

For the first time in days, I laughed out loud. "Yes, as a matter of fact."

I've never cared for being laughed at, not at any age. She gave me a cool look and busied herself running a cloth over the counter. "The future is up to you, girl. It's my job to see that you have one." Behind her the hands of the pocket watch clock were spinning round and round in the wrong direction. My mouth dropped open slightly. The woman's eyes shifted as if she knew what I was looking at but she didn't bother to turn. She smirked.

"When I go out there, will time – "

She interrupted me. "Your friend is waiting for you," she said. "Everyone is."

***

Denise didn't say anything when I came out. She looked like she didn't want to get close to me and the next minute she hugged me and kissed my cheek.

The sunlight hadn't altered at all. Still white hot. Still directly overhead. My eyes teared, tried to close. I concentrated on pulling out onto the highway, heading for home. When the flash came behind us, neither of us looked back.

This is the kind of mechanic I need — the auto repair place that can fix <u>everything</u>. I was probably looking for a one-size-fits-all when I combined time travel and ghost and came up with Mr. Early.

Early's Engine Repair & Auto Body:
We'll Fix It

Morning's just not my time. What can you say about a time of day that makes you feel like a pair of old dirty socks rinsed and hung out over the shower rod in a cheap motel room?

Her voice startles me out of my third or fourth cup of coffee. I look up and she's just there, the way women appear in office doorways in books, not there one minute, there the next. I can't believe I didn't sense her coming. Not someone like her.

She's blond, the kind of blond that pours like honey, the kind of blond you just want to run your hands through. And she's not leaning against the office door, she's standing there kind of quivering, fear or something, but I like the effect. She's one of those girls got side orders of everything that counts and those legs . . .

She startles me again, says the name that used to be my father's and now belongs to me. I stiffen right up, stand and say, "Yes, ma'am," when she says, "Mr. Early?"

I know all the jokes. Yeah, Early. The Late Mr. Early. Early Times. Okay, okay. But I don't tell her to call me Mike, because nobody does. It's always just Early.

She's waiting for me to get my shit together like she's used to it. Probably is. Doesn't help when she licks her lips with just the tip of a pink triangular tongue, but then I notice something else – the lip she's licking is split. And when I look closer, she's not just showing signs of nerves or a couple anxious nights – one of her eyes is definitely ringed with something other than smudged mascara. And I start to get angry before I know anything else but I shove it down where it can't do any harm and ask her into my "office": Early's Engine Repair & Auto Body, Est. 1902. Bring it in, get it on the rack, we'll fix it. Somewhere along the line I got known as a fixer. Sometimes I am.

So I ask her in. If I could do it all over again, hindsight, and all that . .

. . . I'd probably ask her in anyway.

She sits down across the desk from me and I'm pretty sure I'm not going to be giving her an estimate on the cost to fix her tranny. She looks everywhere but at me and I'm just about to ask what her name is when I hear my own voice saying, "Husband trouble?"

I hate it when I do that.

Her lips move, beautiful lips, some kind of pink gloss and I don't think there's a man alive who'd care what they're saying as long as he could watch them move, but I catch up to hear she's answering my question.

And not answering it.

Because I hear her voice: Please, Mr. Early, you've got to help me . . .

And I hear her voice: No, he would never, he slipped, it was an accident . . .

. . . and everything I'm hearing is tonal and wrong, a grating sound that makes my teeth ache.

Ordinarily this is when I'd say, "Have a seat," but she's already sitting and I'm off balance. Ever since she walked in I've felt dizzy, like the back of my head's draining out between my shoulder blades and spinning away down a sink. My ears are ringing like they do at the tail end of a good drunk. I'm not that shy around beautiful women, so I make another attempt to ask her name and manage to bark out "Name!" and she widens her eyes a little but doesn't flinch. Somehow, that bothers me.

Bothers me even more when she says "Melissa" and I hear "Mine, she's mine, she's mine," but Melissa doesn't blink so maybe I can put that one down to imagination.

"You want some coffee?" I'm already on my feet. I need to move. I need more coffee. I need—"

"I need your help, Mr. Early," she says and looks up at me with those killer blue eyes. Christ, almost like a child's eyes they're so big and blue and clear and she can't be more than 28–

–90, she's 90, old and fat and broken–

and whatever is going on in my head, I've got to shut the door on it, shove it down where it can't hurt anything. Before she goes running out of here more afraid of me than whatever drove her to me in the first place. Because she is afraid.

Somehow, knowing that, *understanding* that, puts me back together. All at once I'm back in my body, back on my feet. I can think again, don't feel like I've cornered the market on tequila.

"What kind of car is it?" I ask. I know damn well it isn't, but it might give her a chance to start.

It does. She gives herself a little shake, which does all kinds of nice things for her generous portions and causes me to sit back down behind the desk in a hurry.

"It's not about my car, Mr. Early," she says, giving me an earnest look as if she doesn't think I'm going to get it.

"I didn't think it was," I tell her and sit back in my chair with my fingers laced behind my head. I'd like to put my feet on the desk but that might be going too far. I want to look confident and non-threatening, and the only way to not lean toward that body is to lean away from it.

Then she's up, ranging through the office of Early's Engine Repair and Auto Body which surely could use a woman's touch but that's not what she's got in mind. She just needs to get clear of me for a couple minutes.

Not much to see. Pin up calendar. NASCAR and some women from somewhere. Seals of approval, business license, more calendars, clocks, because for some reason Early's always has multiples of those. Dirty counter, coffee pot, mints in a box with a suggested donation from some civic organization and that whole thing probably dates back to when the earlier Mr. Early was here but fortunately nobody ever wants a mint.

She settles for standing by the glass door, looking out across the parking lot and the cars parked there, waiting for service.

"It's my husband," she says, and I think, "Well, duh. Tell me something I don't know."

Mr. Overconfident. When I blink she's sitting across the desk from me again like she never got up.

"Look," she says. "It's not really very interesting. I don't even know why I came here. Could we just forget . . ."

. . . that she looks like she's 28 and that voice – hers, the one outside of hers, mine, the one I can't identify, the one that says she's 90 and–

"Tell me." She's half risen from the seat when I say this and she looks at me, suddenly afraid, then sinks back down.

And she's right. It's not really an interesting story. It's not unique. It should be, damn it. Nobody has that right. But her story's a small one – great romance, feet sweeping off of, golden carriages and glass slippers and a little girl done good, get thee to a mansion Ophelia and . . .

. . . and then he changed. (Only he didn't, he just showed himself, beauty and the beast, all rolled up into one.)

And then he changed s'more. (Yeah, he probably did, and now you can call *him* Mr. Overconfident, because he thought she'd just lie there and take it and take it and take it, and instead she came to me.)

Started with the usual. A slap here, or there, shocking on its own, but it progressed to Things that Don't Show, and sometimes that scared her because internal bleeding doesn't show. And now . . . now he's not afraid of marking his property. Knows what's his her husband does.

"I can't leave him," she says simply, about the time I open my mouth to ask. Okay, he has more money than God, I was about to say, but it won't do you any good if you're dead, followed by the hype about shelters and counseling and–

"He pays all my sister's medical bills." She looks down at her hands. "We can't live without him. And he's told me if I leave him . . ."

He'll kill you, I think.

"He'll kill my sister." She looks at me to make sure I understand. "And leave me alive."

"Shit," I say, almost impressed, and she nods as if in agreement. "What do you want me to do?" My hands are flat on the desk in front of me, my gaze level with hers as she sits back down across from me. She's still insanely beautiful but now I'm working, and I'm on even keel. Now things are different.

"What do you want me to do?" I ask again. She looks so miserable I feel like a heel, but I *never* make suggestions. They've got to tell me what they want.

"I want you to fix it," she says finally, when she sees I'm not going to jump in, and she mentions a name I know and trust, which also happens to be the motto of my hometown news, a place I never want to see my pretty face.

So I ask again, a little more gently. "What do you want me to do?"

A little defiance then. She looks me in the eye and says, "What do you usually do, Mr. Early?"

"Usually I fix cars, lady," I tell her and stand up like the meeting is over. That makes her eyes go wide and she reaches out toward me.

"I want you to make him stop."

I don't sit back down. "I don't kill people," I tell her. Actually, I do, sometimes. But "fixing" gets me out of trouble long before "killing" would.

She gives me a look I can't read, this side of denial but as if it's not out of the realm of possibility. Or maybe as if I've lost my mind.

Or maybe it is a *perish the thought!* look. Because she gets up and goes out of the office without another word. Morning sun catches the glass door and the words "We'll Fix It!" stand against absolutely nothing for an instant as sunlight occludes everything else. I sigh, because if that's not some kind of sign, what is?

For all the sun, it's freezing outside. I take her coat and purse and we stand in the parking lot and she looks everywhere but at me. Her lip gloss is just as shiny and pink and I wonder how it would taste, but the split in her lip is even more evident out here, and the darkness around one eye before she puts on her sunglasses. She moves stiff and I'm angry again and I say before I can stop myself, "I need his name and some particulars. I'll look into it. Talk to him. Really *talk* to him, if I have to. Okay?"

She nods, still looking east, away from me. She's holding the coat and the purse and shivering, like she's forgotten everything. But she says, "His name's Dan Marino."

Least that's what I hear. I just look at her.

She sighs. "Not that one. Merino." And she spells it, and says, "He's in *business,*" as if it means something, but it doesn't. Better than if he were a cop or something.

"I'm not cheap," I tell her.

She nods again and opens the purse, digs through it and hands me a fat wad of cash, bills all squashed together like discarded tissue. It's way too much money.

"I'm not that expensive." Yeah, I'd like it. But it's enough for that thing I tell people I don't do.

She looks at me directly then. "It's *his* money," she spits, and then she's gone. Flat white glare of morning sun and the sound of an expensive engine that definitely doesn't need me to fix it and I'm standing there cold and holding a bunch of money.

Dan Merino is dead. First guy I go to, Ray, finds things. I fix things, he finds things. I hand over a generous portion of the lady's largesse and

Ray does some magic on the keyboard, stuff I don't even vaguely understand, and comes back and tells me, "Dead on delivery, dude."

I think about Melissa's split lip and shake my head. "No way. He's still hitting people."

Ray glances at the printout in his hand. "Not officially. Officially he's daisies, dude."

Sometimes if you give Ray more money he changes his mind. Didn't look like it this time. "Heart attack?" Maybe he got so angry at Melissa he keeled over and . . .

. . . and what? It happened this morning while I was on my way to Ray's?

Ray looks at the pages in his hand. "That's weird. No cause of death listed. No date, either. I'll look s'more." I take my leave of him.

County offices are overheated, the way I think they're required by law to be. Lady behind the counter doesn't seem to care what information I request as long as I take a number and wait to be called before I do so. We're the only two people in the place, so I get called pretty fast, and the whole thing seems pretty stupid but in keeping with the one-buttoned cardigan and the wispy bun and the glasses.

"I need to know about Dan Merino," I tell her and she gives me a look that says, "I get all the nuts." "Not that one," and I spell it. She gives me another look anyway and produces the file and points at a table across from the desk.

And he turns up dead. Doornail, daises and other things that start with D. And that doesn't make any sense. Because according to her files, he's been dead for at least seven months, since April, and the I look at the date again, but the year is smudged, looks like 35 and that's crazy, must be 05, not that that's particularly sane what with Melissa and her split lip, but I can't think about it because every time I try to look at the DOD, or even the DC, I'm hit with nausea. Vertigo. Roaring in my ears. A drowning sensation like I'm going down, one too many times. So sick I can't walk right but I get the file back to Ms. Spinster and stumble outside.

Outside is a swirl of blue sky and bright pain. Guy's out of nowhere, grabs me by the arm and slams me into the brick wall of the county complex. Everywhere else in the world there'd be cameras, but our municipality decided to respect everyone's right to privacy. So it's a private thump this guy gives my head against the stone.

"Mr. Merino said he's not interested and recommends you aren't either," the thug says. His breath is worse than being battered.

"The football player?" This earns me another good thunk.

"Just step down, asshole." Thunk.

"Mr. Merino is dead," I say experimentally.

"So just stop," the guy says and thunks my head against the wall and then he's gone in a blaze of glory and stars while I try to figure out what happened. And what's happening.

"Your husband's dead," I tell Melissa the next morning when she appears as if we had a standing appointment I've forgotten. "You forgot to mention that."

"Does this look like the work of a man who's dead?" she asks. When she takes off her sunglasses, both eyes are black.

No. It looks like the work of a man who had his goon thunk my head into a wall. She gives me more money and I take it, because this morning when I woke up, everything she'd given me before was gone. I told myself the goon took it.

Merino ran a dry cleaning empire. That's where he got the money she's being so free with. He cleaned up, one could say, though one wouldn't have to.

I try telling her I don't think I can help her. I don't want to end up dead like her husband seems to be. But she's left the glasses off and she looks up at me with those hurt blue eyes and moves her hands uncertainly and I know I'm supposed to take her in my arms and comfort her.

There's no comfort in this embrace. Her breasts press against my chest so soft and round and without any of that underwire and corseting nonsense between us, just female flesh and the thin material of her blouse. I can imagine the way her hips would fit round under my hands. She looks up at me from the circle of my arms, licks still slick pink and I think if Merino is going to kill me, it might as well be for a good reason, and I lean down and taste them, soft, yielding. Dizzy. Sick. For a minute the woman in my arms is thick and solid, blond hair coarsened, a smell stale, and not of perfume.

Then she's gone again and I'm at my desk, feeling my heart racing in places it shouldn't. I can still smell the lipstick but my hands remember a broad, doughy body.

I shiver.

After the techs come in and Sally shows up – late, always late, she stopped making excuses after the first month she worked for me but she's the only one who can figure out everything she's done to the office systems so she's safe as a civil servant – I head to the county again. Different woman, same request. Same results. DC. DOD. 1935. Obviously a typo. Probably DOB. So he was older. Sweet guy.

I'm running out of things to check out. I'm not a PI, I just fix things. Sometimes. And I don't know how to fix this.

I head back over to Ray's with the calm assumption that he'll be home because he's always home. He's either a hacker or has a trust fund, though his Mountain Dew habit sometimes makes me wonder.

"Dan Merino," I say when he lets me in.

"Dude."

"Everything says he's dead." Not that I've checked that many other places.

"Dude, *I* said he was dead." He looks hurt so I hand over the 6-pack of Dew I brought and another handful of Melissa's money. He takes them both like a god accepting tributes and stands waiting for me to tell him what I want.

I don't know what I want. My head still hurts from being thunked. "Could you just see what you can find?" I wave one hand toward his kitchen table where there's something like six computers and parts of others.

Ray looks at me speculatively. "What're you checking out?"

Fair enough. "Domestic situation. His wife–"

"Wife." He comes down hard on the last word but it's still a question. Confused, I nod.

"What about her?"

"He's knocking her around. Or . . . he was. He . . . look, she asked me–"

Ray's eyebrows threaten his hairline. *"She* asked you? She's still alive?"

Now being confused is getting old. "What are you talking about?"

Ray looks at me like I'm an idiot. "She'd be about, what, a hundred?"

This time I just look at him so Ray goes to one of the computers and does something magic on the keyboard and pops up pretty much the same document I was looking at under the scrutiny of Ms. Spinster yesterday. "Did you *see* the date of death, man?"

Briefly the nausea hits again, hard enough for me to swallow several times and to hold onto my stomach like pressing the outside will keep the inside in. Because when he says that I'm hit all over again with nausea and vertigo and that swimming, underwater feeling. I can't even hear him when he starts talking so I push him aside and look at the DC myself and there it is: Date of Death.

1935.

Ray's moved over to another computer while I'm standing there gawping and he motions me over. "Look," and there in a newspaper online morgue is a short obit, Dan Merino, 35 in 1935, and he left behind a 27-year-old widow and yeah, she really would be pushing a hundred, pushing hard at it, but this is all impossible.

I head back to the garage and no one stops to thunk me along the way. On the drive it occurs to me that maybe the dead Merino is the father of the other Merino and I laugh out loud because that makes so much sense. I call Ray when I get there and ask him to check it out but he only comes up with one Dan Merino, married to Melissa, same SSN she gave me, same everything. But dead. A long time ago.

"Man, I would get untangled from this if I were you," Ray says. "Merino was one seriously mean dude, and the money you gave me's disappeared again."

There's no "again" for me because he didn't tell me the first money disappeared but I know what he's talking about.

Donna comes over that night like she sometimes does. Donna's no Melissa but she looks nice in the long dress she cocktails in and better out of it. Standing in my bedroom in that pale peach slip of hers, breasts threatening to spill out of it and all her dips and hollows outlined in silk, she makes me catch my breath. But when I put my arms around her and her breasts press against my naked chest, suddenly I'm seeing Melissa again, then feeling Melissa in my arms, older, thicker, wrinkled Melissa. I start violently and try to let go of her but Donna pushes her face up to mine to be kissed and suddenly the only thing I can identify are those bright blue eyes because everything else is wrinkles and age and a smell I can't identify that's got to be age and dusty despair and decay.

Donna leaves early that night, flushed, but not glowing.

I make an early night of it (some people would find that uproarious) and get a full seven hours of sleep deprivation, of half-dreams my heart pounds through and a feeling there's something I'm supposed to be doing.

Morning's a relief until I go outside and Merino's message man slams me into the side of the house. Siding doesn't feel any better than brick did.

"Mr. Merino. Wants. You. To. Stop," Goon Breath says, driving in each word with a poke of his index finger into my chest.

"Merino's dead, isn't he?" I ask and if his hired hand would stop bouncing my head I could see if he's really wearing spats like I think he is.

"That's for him to know and you—" thud "to find—" thud "out."

"No thanks." Knee to groin because I'm really sick of this and then because I just don't want to see Melissa again, I call Roberto and tell him to hold down the fort at the garage and I take a jaunt to the library and get the woman there who looks like the twin sister of the spinster at the county to show me the microfiche ropes and I look up everything I can on Dan and Melissa Merino.

And it's there. Some of it. Damned cold in the library and I'm chilled to the bone as I read about Dan Merino's short life and his dry cleaning empire and his gangland connections, his petty crime and sudden death and the questionable heart attack that sounds more like he was executed in a hail of Tommy Gun fire.

And his wife. Melissa Merino. Who at 27 survived her husband and went on to do good works with his money and who everyone always suspected had been badly abused by the man, to the point of near death, but who had survived into the 21st century and still, apparently, did.

The microfiche rolls and there's a photo of a woman in her 90s and I shudder at the mouth I almost kissed last night, the mouth I kissed at the garage, the soft pink lips on that ancient haggard face.

I jump about three feet when the librarian sneaks up behind me and lays one hand on my shoulder and she apologizes in that way some women have of making it seem like it was all your fault anyway and all your fault they had to apologize and then she tells me she's got one more batch of film: my other request, cross referencing Merino, Melissa and me.

And there's a picture, though I wish there wasn't. It shows me, at the garage, standing beside Dan Merino, with Melissa just to the side, staring off away from the camera, and a couple people in the background, working, or pretending to, and the caption "From better times: Michael Early, right, has agreed to testify against former friend and gangland kingpin Dan Merino in exchange for immunity. It is rumored Merino's wife, Melissa, pictured far right, will also testify and that she is suing for divorce."

And one more file. And I don't want to look. But curiosity, or fear, gets the better of me.

No photo this time. Just as well. It'd be a morgue shot. Just the headlines. I don't need much more. "Former Friend of Mob Boss found Dead." And my name. And my age.

There's probably more than one Michael Early out there.

Yeah, right, asshole.

And I think I must still be at the library. But it smells and sounds like the garage. And when the hand comes down on my shoulder I don't jump or look around. I can smell her perfume and I know who it is. The hand on my shoulder is young and white and unblemished.

I look again at the microfiche picture. Michael Early, found dead. 1935. My heart pounds strong in my chest. I turn off the viewer, return the spools to the librarian and drive back to the garage. There's work I can do there while I wait.

The Late Mr. Early, shot down by his one-time friend before he could testify. Was it because of her? I can't remember, I think, but I can. The peach-colored slip, the bountiful breasts straining against the lace cups. The way she watched me with those blue, blue eyes. That mouth and the pink lipstick.

But I'm still 33. I'm still young and strong. I'm still alive, I can effect what's around me. If I can effect it, I can change it. I'm a fixer. That's what I do. Sometimes. I fix things.

Sooner or later Melissa will come. Or Merino's thug, or Merino himself. They have to come, before I can really figure out what's going on.

And fix it.

I settle back to wait.

I started writing this story with the intention of submitting it to an open call anthology looking for ghost stories and police work, which predated the 2013 R.I.P.D. movie by several years. The story stalled on me and the anthology closed and a very long time and several projects later I ran across the pages I'd written and finished it. Even though I wrote it, the resulting story still gives me the creeps.

On the Squad

Suspended, without pay. Apparently the Santa Esmeralda PD preferred its officers without hallucinations.

Thomas Decker did, too. He protested. Hired a union rep. Hired an attorney. He said the same thing over and over: Take me off this detail.

He'd already worked the Dead Squad longer than anyone in the history of the PD had worked it – he started it, worked it since his unfortunate incident started the whole thing and how did SEPD repay its best and its brightest? Suspended. Without pay.

"Look at it from their point of view," Lisa said that night. She stood behind the reclining couch and rubbed the muscles in his neck which were appreciative but non-responsive. They'd gone hard and angry and had no intention of relaxing until Thomas did.

"Why in the hell would I want to do that?"

He sounded particularly snarly. He tried not to snarl at Lisa, but –

"Well," she said thoughtfully, thumbs digging into the hard places on his neck, "this is Santa Esmeralda Police Department. SEPD. And by shipping you off to psych – or just off – you become somebody else's problem. SEP."

Thomas thought about that for a minute. "What's the D stand for?"

"Damn it? Dummy? Delegated?"

"I knew there was a reason I married you."

"Because I can make acronyms?"

And she went off into the kitchen to start dinner, apparently not that concerned that he wasn't going to be working for the next two weeks.

Thomas was. Two weeks was a lifetime without The Job. Two weeks was a lifetime even with the job – ever since the job turned bad.

***

He was on the couch again at two a.m. No point keeping Lisa awake just because he couldn't sleep. Maybe tonight it would just be good old-fashioned insomnia. He could take that. He sat on the couch and stared into the living room, looking carefully into every shadowy corner. Nothing there. Nothing to worry about. The lights from the fan-chandelier combination overhead warmed the room. White light, not a bit ecologically green. He had a book, something Lisa'd put down out of boredom. He turned on the stereo, very low, Rolling Stones driving back a little more of the dark.

OK, this could be all right. He couldn't sleep but thanks to being SEPD's SEP, D, he didn't have to get up tomorrow morning.

Thomas read. Dove into the book. Overlooked the overabundance of cats in the plot and just read.

And slowly, with dread, slid up out of the text.

Someone was watching him. Standing there in his empty, night-dark living room. The one where the light should have been abusing the environment and illuminating everything.

Thomas didn't make a sound. He didn't shift on the couch. He kept the paperback up. He wanted more than anything not to look up.

He looked up.

Rusty Evans stood there, face pale from lack of blood. Blood drained away when the head was severed and it seemed just because Rusty had reattached his hadn't stopped the sort of rampant anemia.

"Please." He didn't know he'd spoken aloud until his voice released Rusty and allowed him to speak.

"Help me."

Thomas shot off the couch. The world spun, nauseating, too fast and too hot.

"I can't. I *can't*. I can't do this anymore. Please, Rusty, I know you got a bad deal – "

Everyone said Rusty Evans was a bad cop.

Now he could see the hole in Rusty's chest. If he tried, he could remember every instant and every event, every insult to the body that led to Rusty's death.

He hadn't been there. He hadn't even known Rusty, who worked for the county's consolidated drug taskforce.

No worries. By virtue of speaking he'd loosened Rusty's tongue.

By acknowledging him, he'd freed the specter to speak.

By awareness he'd dragged home the story.

"I won't. I *can't*. It's too much." *I didn't even know you, man.*

If he just denied. If he just refused.

He closed his eyes, a leap of faith he only made because the terror was too great, the exhaustion and fear. Because he didn't want to be SEP, he wanted to be SEPD. He'd started the damn ghost squad, hadn't meant to, hadn't had a clue what he was doing and no idea how to stop it before it drove them all mad.

He closed his eyes in denial and the ice of the ghost slashed through him.

When he could open his eyes again, the living room was empty.

No point going to bed now. He'd only wake Lisa when the inevitable dreams came.

He switched off the Stones and turned on the television.

The screaming started at dawn. Streaks of orange light lit the California sky when he woke shouting. From deep in the house Lisa came running, swearing and banging into walls. Thomas rocked up in the recliner, trying to pull away from the dreams.

They weren't dreams.

Before she could reach him he got off the couch and over to the kitchen sink, couldn't make it any farther before everything he'd ever eaten spewed up out of him. The hairs on his arms and the back of his neck stood. The malignancy coursed through him, rage and blood and pain, Rusty's terror and sorrow and the killer's mal intent.

The killers on paper were teenaged boys already sentenced to spend their next several lifetimes in jail and the courts didn't fuck around when it came to sentencing and following through on cop killers.

The actual killer would never be caught. Even with the formation of the Ghost Squad and the officers on it SEPD was calmly watching go insane, cops and courts weren't going to be able to accept.

Ghosts – revenants and hauntings – yes.

Demons?

He didn't think so.

"What did you see?"

In the morning sunlight that was such a ridiculous question. Lisa sat across their glass-topped rock and iron table in the early morning sunlight, her blond hair brassy, her green eyes narrowed as if she intended to ferret out the information she wanted using the serrated grapefruit spoon she now pointed at him. "I want to know what you saw."

Sunlight hit the glass tabletop and dazzled him. His eyes teared up and he let them. Easier than blinking tears away, making a cover story. "No. Lisa, love, I appreciate that you want to help me but this – "

"Is killing you." She paused a long time before she must have judged he wasn't going to go on. "You need to do something before you're prey to your own ghost squad."

That day he felt good and truly haunted. Every half-glimpsed reflection in a mirror was Rusty Evans. Every object he reached for that turned out to be out of place had been moved there by supernatural means. Rusty died a hideous death, beaten and finally beheaded by a pack of meth head dealer teens. Of course he was restless. Of course he couldn't settle.

But something else was happening. Something outside the norm which was nothing approaching normal as it was.

Death bed confessions went by the wayside once death scene cops were on hand.

"It's just being around it," he told Lisa in the beginning. "And maybe sun spots."

She'd grinned, a bright green-eyed blond and goofy Lisa smile, the way she used to.

Thomas Decker was the first SEPD officer with the gift. Standing at the scene of a triple homicide, mother and daughters, father in custody, case more open and shut than anyone liked, he stepped out of the bloody sea of salt heat in the bedroom. Most of the evidence already collected. Most of the assumptions already made. Police and coroner's people all over the place when he went down the hall to one of the kid's rooms, found himself sitting on a chair much too small for him, just taking a couple breaths.

She sat down across from him and he didn't recognize her. She wore a sweatshirt and jeans but it was the middle of the night. Decker wouldn't have been overly surprised if SEPD started sending shock and PTSD counselors on scene to deal with cops still trying to initially process the scene.

It was a very touchy-feely department that way.

In the long run, the touchy-feely aspect of SEPD saved his ass. Because they were willing to listen when Thomas Decker said he'd seen a ghost and that she'd told him who killed her.

"This is my daughter's room," she said by way of introduction when he didn't speak first.

Decker pushed back away from the table so hard the little chair went flying. He scrambled up from the floor and kept his distance from the blond in the sweatshirt. Now he could see the blood in her hair, the bulging right eye, the teeth visible through the torn cheek on the right side. A tire iron does terrible things to flesh.

The blond waited, not offended by his reaction, but not apologetic, either. When the panic receded enough for him to understand her, she nodded in the direction of the closet. The louvered doors were pulled closed behind a Hello, Kitty! Poster. Coat hangers swung from the louvers with school clothes hanging on out of sheer perversity.

"I had three daughters, Detective Decker," the murdered woman said quietly.

There had been two blond bodies in the bed beside her.

"My other daughter is in the closet. She's very afraid." She looked long and longingly at the closet but didn't approach. "She can't see me." She stared at him with very blue eyes. "I don't know why you can."

He found his voice. "I thought you were a cop. Police psychiatrist."

She laughed at that. An unfortunate little laugh, the kind made by someone who doesn't expect to laugh again for a long time. Then she grew serious and leaned forward as if sharing a secret.

"My husband did not do this, Detective Decker. He is not having an affair. He did not want to be free of his family." She paused, looked again toward the closet where her daughter hid, and then behind her at the open bedroom door and the stairs beyond leading down where her husband waited in custody. "My sister Clem is schizophrenic, Detective. That's short for Clementine, though she doesn't like to be called that. Clem did this." She waved one hand at her face, then turned her head and spat a mouthful of blood that flared into light and vanished before it hit the floor. "Clem is my twin, Detective. When you find her you'll find DNA stunningly like mine. I didn't do this. My husband didn't do this. Clem did. And before she managed to get hold of Jennica – " One last look toward the closet – "Please. Find her. You'll find the evidence you need."

He had. Starting with the daughter, the one hiding in the closet who now lived with her dad in a much smaller house, having a much smaller life. Clem, who'd left her own traces everywhere, was in a facility for the criminally insane.

And Decker, after having been ferreted out by a real police psychiatrist and having won the case and started the ghost squad, had gone on to be suspended without pay. Because with Rusty Evans' death, something other than the truth started coming through, and that was more than SEPD wanted to know.

"What do you want for dinner?" Lisa asked, standing in the doorway to his home office. The fact that he didn't want anything wouldn't cut it with her. It would just make her feel more guilty about leaving him to go to some women's networking thing.

He had no idea why she went. Lisa taught first grade. She didn't need to network and most of her friends taught also. She had yet to accept any of the invitations to head (up/down) to the bay area to shop for professional clothes in consignment shops and usually wore nice jeans to work. When the school district requested she keep the jeans for Fridays, Lisa had pointed out the long hours and low pay and number of teachers not beating down the school district's door, then asked what they intended to do about it. So she didn't use the networking group for shopping for professional clothes. Thomas had finally reached the conclusion she went to networking groups to remind herself of all the jobs she could be stuck with.

Like wife of a cop going crazy.

"Just thaw me out a pork chop. I'll have it with green beans."

Behind Lisa in the hall, something moved. Thomas darted forward before he could stop himself and yanked her aside. Lisa made a sound of distress and caught herself against the door frame.

There was nothing behind her. Just a framed painting, the glass catching the light spilling out of his office. Maybe Lisa had moved, and the glass had caught her reflection.

Thomas ran a hand over his face. "I'm so sorry."

She nodded, and stroked his arm, and said she'd thaw out some chops and there was a steamer package of green beans and some nice merlot opened. But she stood on her tiptoes to kiss his cheek and she didn't offer to stay home with him and there was a distance there he'd never sensed before.

"You probably hate being off the job," she said as she stood by the front door putting on her coat. "But maybe a break is exactly what you need."

He noticed her blond hair seemed in disarray, the back of it scrunched as if she'd been sleeping on it. He frowned a little, and brushed at it, then settled the collar of her coat and cupped her face in his hands. Lisa leaned her head to one side, kissed his palm and pulled away faster than she might once have done.

"Are you getting any sleep?" he asked. Just because he got up and went into the living room and for the most part stopped screaming then didn't mean she wasn't lying awake worrying about him.

"I'm fine," she lied, and kissed him again and went out the front door.

He turned on the porch light and she turned to look back and Thomas saw a shadow move across her face, something that shouldn't have been there. Something that made her look like something else, old and wizened, terrifyingly wrong. "Be careful," he said, and she smiled, with teeth somehow too sharp. And Thomas went back inside too quickly and watched mindless TV until she came home hours later with equally mindless gossip about people he didn't know and projects she wasn't part of and an offer he didn't even try to refuse.

And for a while he slept without screaming.

Rusty Evans stood in front of him in the night-dark bedroom. Thomas had shot awake so hard his muscles ached. Beside him, Lisa hadn't wakened, so he stayed still, trying not to bother her.

Just Rusty, head looking not quite put back on right.

Rusty had a wife. Kids. A house in a middle-aged neighborhood.

Raw deal.

That wasn't why he was there.

Thomas stood, sliding out of bed and coming to his feet fluidly. Lisa slept on. In the uncertain light of the bedroom where the streetlight crept in through the blinds, her face looked normal.

Thomas jerked his head at Rusty, went up the hall and into his office where he turned on all the lights, including the $80 UV/ion thing that was supposed to keep them from being depressed when coastal clouds rolled in midwinter.

Rusty didn't waver and vanish in the light. The old time nightmares of childhood had been vastly preferable to the reality of ghost squad. Turn on a light for a childhood nightmare and all the boogeymen vanished.

"Why are you here?

Rusty spread his hands, reasonable but not communicating. All very sad. He'd been undercover. He'd been set up. He wasn't a dirty cop. Wasn't.

Only Thomas didn't believe that. He didn't really want Rusty Evans to know he didn't believe that, but he didn't. Because a raw deal meant Thomas went to SEPD – which he did – and made a ghost squad report that the two teenaged dealers accused of killing Rusty hadn't – which he had done.

The real perp, the machete-wielding psycho wholesaler, was on a most wanted list, and Rusty assured justice.

But Rusty wasn't gone.

Which meant justice wasn't what Rusty was looking for.

"I can't help you if you won't tell me what you want." Turning back to the specter. In time to see something utterly wrong, some inside out thing of fang and violence.

Thomas jolted back, stumbled on the office chair and sat down quickly. The rollers engaged and the chair scuttled back to the wall where it perched against a bookcase. The thing that should have been Rusty Evans grinned at Thomas Decker and slid upward through the ceiling.

Thomas sat staring at the ceiling where the thing had gone.

There were other reasons why the dead stayed. Most of the time the reasons made sense. Most of the time there seemed to be a logic to the appearances. Show up at a crime scene, the victim or victims would talk to the first responding officer, and when that didn't work, wait for ghost squad. If the whole thing was obvious – drunk driver kills self and no one else in a single car accident, of example – someone from ghost squad went along. To hear confession, as it were. Sometimes to take word to the family – he was sober, a rabbit ran into the road; he swerved, or, Apologies, if he had it to do over …

Not always. People, unfortunately, were people. Some stayed around to pass on messages of venom and rage. At first ghost squad tried to simply censor those, refusing to relay them. The resulting hauntings made it more worthwhile to simply adjust the language, pass on the sentiments and move the fuck on.

Thomas had relayed a few he'd particularly enjoyed, to an employer who'd fired a long term company man in favor of his nephew. The message – *I'll be waiting for you, and we'll see how even the playing field is then* – had seemed fairly innocuous but the jowly, self-assured rat's ass of an employer had paled perceptibly and sweated a lot.

So. Rusty Evans. Not ready to move on. Not ready to talk about it.

That wasn't the problem. The problem was Rusty was *haunting* Thomas. Who'd been trying to help him.

Night still pressed against the windows. Thomas had developed an intense hatred for nighttime. But he missed sleeping pressed up against Lisa without every light burning. He left his office, made his way up the hall and through the dark bedroom without too many incidents involving vulnerable body parts and misplaced inanimate objects, and crawled in beside his wife. She was warm and soft and sleep scented and made a noise of query without waking. Thomas said, "Shh," and held her and closed his eyes, and slept.

He woke without screaming, terrified so thoroughly from sleep he couldn't make a sound. Gray dawn light was just beginning to creep through the closed blinds. Convulsively he reached for Lisa, his flailing hand going high and wide. He encountered flesh.

About three feet above where it should have been.

His eyes snapped open. Terror drummed inside him. When he fought free of the blankets he saw her clearly.

Lisa hovered above the bed, hovering, horrifyingly aloft. Her pajamas had twisted tight around her, binding, constricting. Her limbs spasmed out from her body, hard, rigid, hands twisted into ancient, arthritic-looking claws. Her joints all looked wrong, twisted, unnatural, stiff as if she were caught in extreme seizure.

Convulsion. Her face twisted tight, a grimace as her eyes moved violently back and forth under closed lids. She dreamed, clearly some nightmare from which she couldn't wake.

He wanted to grab for her, pull her back down to the bed, as though he'd wakened to find her engaged in some foolish but normal pastime, balancing on a step stool placed atop kitchen chairs so she could just get the cobwebs off the light fixture, it isn't like I'm going to fall, take a breath already.

Levitating, his mind screamed, she's levitating, and no matter how much he wanted to reach for her he found himself taking a step back, stumbling off the edge of the bed. He caught himself on the books stacked there, lost his balance and pinwheeled backward. He caught up against the wall hard, sending one of the framed prints shattering onto a bedside table, rattling the window.

Waking Lisa.

Something opened her eyes.

Lisa screamed.

Something inside Lisa laughed.

It was Lisa's body, and somewhere inside, her mind and soul. He forced himself back to the bed, looking away from too bright, too old eyes, from the mouth with too many too sharp teeth. Everything was exaggerated, the sunlight coming through the Venetian blinds, the clarity of the room, the edges to objects. Lisa. The thing inside Lisa.

When he reached for her, her skin burned, fever hot. Stove top hot. Thomas grabbed her wrists. Tension shot through her body. Her muscles coiled, hard. Rigid. Her limbs were immovable.

The thing inside glinted and glared.

Thomas met her eyes. Met its eyes. And past the rage and malice and glee, he saw Lisa, and fear, and despair.

So he used gentleness to pull her from her impossible perch. He kept his voice steady and ignored his own words, knew only that he was saying her name and the word love over and over, in between telling her what he meant to do. As if he knew. Somehow he didn't think telling his plans would make any difference. Whatever was inside her knew what he had in mind.

He would drag it out of Lisa. Send it away. Exorcize. Disperse.

In his arms, on the bed, Lisa whimpered. Argued. Soft agreement in puffs of stolen air between exhortations from the thing. Death. Loss. Damnation.

Rusty Evans was a bad cop. Rusty Evans did this to you. Rusty Evans let this free. Rusty Evans –

"Shut up," Thomas told the thing inside Lisa and despite the foul reek coming from her mouth, put his lips over hers and used everything between them to call her back.

He called back Rusty Evans instead.

The dead officer stood on the far side of the bed where the early morning eastern sun found a wrong-turned slat in the Venetian blinds. Dust motes in the sunlight showed clearly. So did Rusty Evans. He looked whole and solid, alive, as if he'd made some decision and, in doing so, realized himself somehow.

Thomas's automatic shields went up. Bad cop. He believed that now. Rusty Evans was a bad cop. Bad kill. Thomas wasn't willing to understand the haunting. Rusty Evans had received all the justice care of Thomas

Decker that he was going to. His true killers on most wanted programs. The two kids on reduced charges for their actual crimes. And Rusty Evans, bad cop, was not Thomas Decker's problem anymore.

Rusty Evans needed to be SEP.

Rusty nodded. In the morning light his eyes looked resigned, sad, not angry. The open chest, headless specter had gone. Rusty stood out of uniform, in a t-shirt and jeans. Briefly Thomas saw his children around him, two little boys and a girl, all redheads like their father. And that memory was brushed away by Rusty, who moved forward, reaching for Lisa where she lay rigid and lost in Thomas' arms.

For just an instant, Thomas stiffened, and then he relaxed, though he didn't loosen his hold.

Rusty moved gently, unwillingly, reaching out to place one hand over Lisa's mouth, the other just above her breasts. His arm brushed Thomas's and Thomas flinched. Rusty had shape and substance.

And then Rusty was only important in relation to Lisa, because he'd said something Thomas had missed, something about *come back* or *I surrender* or *you can* or *I won't fight* or maybe, impossibly, he'd said all of it at once, and also something about being a better host, the violence, the job.

Lisa arched, hard, her body bending back until Thomas lost his grip on her, scrabbling after her on the bed as she bent as if meaning to touch the back of her head to her heels. S he made one sudden, powerful sound and then cried out in pain. Something shot from her mouth, something made of flame and smoke, ash and anger.

Lisa screamed.

The thing tore from her, coiling, arrowing upward, taking on speed and killing force before it plunged, hard, sharp, fast, for Rusty Evans, who stood with arms spread wide, accepting.

The demon slammed into Rusty.

Rusty closed his eyes briefly, opened them, and grinned at Thomas as if he'd just done something tremendously wonderful.

Through clenched teeth, he said, "I win," and nodded, and reached out one hand to touch Thomas Decker's forehead.

The vision tore through him. Of Rusty, at a crime scene, standing over the victim but this time the victim was a rapist, shot by his intended victim who stood a few feet away, shivering, giving her statement, drinking bad coffee while yellow police tape went up all around her in the parking garage where she'd been attacked.

Rusty, standing over the victim, a ghost squad cop who saw the specter start to rise and prepared for the vision or confession or accusation or whatever would come.

Not prepared for the possession.

In the breath before the scream – *I didn't do it!* – the thing came from the body, blasting up out of it and into Rusty's open mind that waited to receive a message. It came, filling him, taking him. Drowning him deep down within himself.

Rusty Evans died that day, almost a year before an undercover assignment put him in the way of a psycho methhead with a machete. Almost a year before accusations that he was a bad cop ripped away his family and made his back up hesitate just long enough that shots were fired, and a blade was swung.

"I'll tell them," Thomas said, cradling Lisa, but reaching for Rusty. "I'll tell everyone."

And Rusty Evans grinned again, keeping his teeth tight together, keeping the demon back inside and Thomas saw when the thing started to understand how it had been caught, started to battle against Rusty for release, looking for the new host it had so recently claimed.

"Too late," Rusty said between clenched teeth. "I win." And he let go, his solid body becoming immaterial, dissipating into a nothing that lingered briefly, dark in the sunlight, like smoke, then vanished.

Lisa sagged against Thomas, sobbing, and he kept his arm around her as he moved through the bedroom, opening blinds and windows.

SEPD did not want to know about demons. It wasn't happy about ghost squad, never had been, only tolerated the freaky shit because it couldn't be disproved. And because it got results. But command brought in a PSI IAD. Thomas's vision was reviewed and the verdict rendered in his favor. Psych eval said he was fit for duty, a bit traumatized from finding Rusty Evans beheaded but anyone would be. He was reinstated, with back pay, and a transfer, if he wanted it, out of ghost squad.

Thomas opted to stay, with the option of transferring at a later date. He might not like the crime scene visions and he might wish he'd never founded ghost squad, but he wasn't quite ready for it all to be somebody else's problem.

What if you could see the future — and no one listened?

The Last Oracle

Show's over, and everyone's heading out, audience and entertainers alike, though she's never sure which is which. For Cassie, watching the crowds is sometimes as much show as what goes on in the canvas and sawdust.

She's on the edges anyway, usually free of the attentions of the ringmaster but not free. So while the show goes on, she watches and listens and hones her craft. She long ago learned to tell the stories they want to hear and to close herself off to the stories they can't. The pounding in her temples no longer comes, no loss of self, no momentary fragmentation. This is her gift to herself. Her gift to them is hope. She's learned to read it on their faces, the way they stand, their clothes and words and wants and maybe there still is just a little bit of spark showing through. But most nights, no one asks for spark. Some nights, no one asks for anything at all.

She dreams of the day the ringmaster will set her free. But they're only dreams, with no shelf life. No spark.

"Long night," said one of the jugglers. Harlequin, him and her. Twins, Cassie learned, white haired and whip thin and bizarre as anyone else in the troupe. Which makes them normal here. The boy is talking to her.

"Not so long. You did good tonight." She watched them, blood-letters, and everyone thinks it's slight of hand, imagery and smoke and mirrors and nothing else, the way the twins use blades on each other while knife jugglers behind them entertain with carefully staged near misses. But there's no illusion to the twins. Lin still licks blood from his hand, his own or his sister's. That's what they come to see, those who come to the big top– not Cassie and her cracked and scarred crystal ball, a prop from the moment she arrived. What she saw, she saw without props. What she saw no one ever listened to, and she'd seen so much across the years.

"What?" She hasn't been listening. The boy usually tells the same sorts of tales anyway.

"I said, here they come."

There are the usual tonight, the ones who try the games of chance, win a teddy bear (free at just over three times the store price when you get done with the dollar-a-tries), a goldfish, an ashtray. The posters, the t-shirts– the ringmaster shirts sell very well. The cost is low and the t-shirts are harmless.

"You will find the love you have always dreamed of. The future is bright." Cassie smiled because the woman in front of her looked incapable of it. Dark, dark eyes, no rings, and the first strands of gray creeping in. She smiled back at Cassie, then, and so it was insight rather than foresight once again.

After the woman they came more scattered, more spread out. A couple children and children always wanted their fortunes told and they were always easy– children, she found, didn't want things, or, at least, the things they wanted were bright and shiny and easily replaced in the mind's eye. They didn't *want* things the way adults did. A young couple came by, husband gently scathing, wife shushing, but he probably believed more than she did. Older woman, very old man.

Not as old as I am, Cassie thought. *I win.*

Until they were gone, big top quiet as though everyone whispered but it was only the night and day difference of crowd, no crowd.

"I'll tell you your future," Lin scoffed as they broke down her booth. "More like I'll tell you what you want. Isn't that all a future is? Wants?"

"Hush," Cassie said gently. He was new. He didn't understand.

"Lin, are you coming?" Mia stood just off to the side by the games of chance, watching them. "Hi, Cassie." The girl looked wan and pale, more washed out than usual. Next to her Lin looked like the sun to his sister's moon.

"Yeah, coming, I guess." But he didn't move, stood with Cassie as if the two of them waited, and in another minute, after Mia had turned and gone, they heard voices. Three women came from the big top, stragglers, walking with their arms linked, talking animatedly. Cassie's booth lay in component parts, but her crystal still stood on its stand, the starred cloth lay around it. She had her stool. She could make do. Every circus has a

fortune teller– she was de rigueur and would be paid whether anyone
wanted a fortune or not, but tips would be nice. There was an international
store just around the corner and a bottle of Ouzo she wanted to pick up
before they headed out tomorrow. The women caught sight of Cassie,
flanked by the twins, and made a beeline for her. Cassie smiled just about to
speak– "Tell your fortune? Read your future?"– when the pain hit. All the
more crippling because she hadn't felt it for so many years, the pain of True
Sight. She took a breath. Get the vision out, get it *said*.

The women spoke first. Their voices, a harmonic, merged into one.
"Tell your fortune?" they asked. "Read your future?"

The dam broke and the vision spilled out all around her. Cassie felt
Lin and Mia grab her arms, to keep her upright. She swayed under their
hands.

Shattering glass, pieces flying. A woman's face reflected in the glass,
someone she didn't recognize. A scream. A sound.

Cassie shuddered and surfaced. "Someone close to you," she
managed. Her throat felt raw and swollen. "Beware. Be careful. There's
glass, and a scream. A wreck, perhaps. She didn't look like any of you."
Her words came faster and faster. Desperate to relay. Desperate to warn.

"Cassie," said the trio of voices. "Nobody listens."

No one ever listened. No one ever had. She had slept the night in the
temple, had made the sacrifices required. Blood sacrifice, blood on her
hands. But just before dawn he had slid in beside her, sun god leading the
day, his breath soft against her neck as the serpents had been when they
whispered their gifts, and he asked one more of her, a god's privilege, the
one thing she would not give, and when she refused him he cursed the gift
and left her for eternities: she may see the future.

But no one will listen.

Lin took her back to her trailer, caring as a mother, protective as a
lover. He undressed her and rubbed the fear sweat from her body with
warm soft rags. His hands were gentle; his eyes were too full.

"Let me stay," he whispered as he eased her back into the skinny single
bed. There was blood on his upper lip where Mia had bitten him. There
was no room between the twins for anyone else. "Let me stay with you,"
Lin whispered again.

Cassie remembered the temple, remembered herself against the dark
stone. She had turned away then, from soft whispers and caresses. She
turned away again. She was pure, then; chaste now. She was a vessel. Some

day, she told herself, she'd find a way to make them listen.

"Let me stay."

"Please, Lin," she said. Too exhausted to say more. She turned away from him and slept.

The night filled with dreams. Not visions or wishes, but memories. Over and over cities fell and lovers died and buildings collapsed and people lost their lives. Cassie thrashed, tangled in covers and effectively bound. She had returned to the temple time after time across the years, as temple became church became street became business became unrecognizable in this time and place. She had begged and pleaded and offered herself: take the gift or remove the curse. Let them listen. Let me warn. Let me be heard.

When she woke in the morning sunlight flooded the trailer. Light through the small dirty windows silhouetted the ringmaster and lit his mane of silver hair.

"Where do you think you would go?" he asked when he saw she was awake. No recriminations. Not angry. But steel underneath. Deadly killing steel.

Cassie looked away from him, looked down at her hands. "Away," she said quietly. "Home." But her words came out "death" and "cold." As always with the ringmaster, her mind filled with visions. She saw him burn, the big top on fire and the flames leaping skyward. She saw him fall, pushed, plunging from the top of the circus tent, his neck snapped on impact. She saw him stabbed and shot and run through in duels, saw him falling and burning and poisoned and shot. Her head reeled with vertigo and un-truth. Always lies with the ringmaster, always un-truths. Always others in his place. How many years ago had she tried to stop the circus fire that killed so many? She was almost listened to then– some got out, and safe. But in the doing she had encountered the ringmaster and he had snared her. An exchange: her services as performer and in return he'd cut the show short, send them away before they burned.

He'd only partially lied– he sent them away before the burning took hold but not before the smoke caught some and the flames caught others, not in time to save them all, only in time to keep his bargain and seal her fate. But she'd lied too– because the services she'd promised him, the skill and talent, drifted and waned the moment she was near him. She was as much trapped by her own need as by his promise: when she was near him the visions no one listened to were stilled.

"Will you let me go?" she asked. "Will you set me free?"

And he laughed, and was gone, although she could not remember hearing the trailer door open and close; she was alone again.

The women were back again that night. Two hundred miles later in another town, after a performance wracked with falls and problems. Cassie had seen them all. She hadn't even tried to say anything. The ringmaster understood her. The ringmaster heard her when she spoke. But it was his ring, his circus, his big top. His problem, she sighed, and had anything of major proportions threatened even he wouldn't have heard her.

Post performance she saw two small children— "Will I get a puppy for my birthday?" and there was a spark there, just a tiny one, and yes, you will get your heart's desire, though she rather thought it looked more like a rabbit than a puppy, and the other, can you make my mother send my baby brother back? and that just made her laugh. A handful of adults looking for love or just asking for entertainment's sake or, one of them, looking for missing keys and there was a moment's bright pain when she located them. It was coming back. Unbidden. Unasked. Lin stood behind her while she read and when he reached out and touched her the spark leapt and she was flushed with pain and vision. Family, family car, interstate trucker, she saw the collision and said, "Don't take the freeway home, take the back roads." The father snorted and threw crumpled ones at her, tugging his wife away by the wrist, but the wife's eyes believed. Maybe he'd listen to her if not to Cassie.

The women came late, the very last of the stragglers. They were all very dark, like Cassie's own people, dark and full lipped and walking again with their arms linked as if they were one being. Lin went still at the sight of them, a cat judging a potential threat.

"Cassie. We see you. We hear you. You can be free."

"*How?*" Free from which? From the ringmaster and the promise that kept her bound? Already the visions were returning but to walk away condemned the crowd from how many hundreds of years ago? The crowd with her one-time husband and child, one of the families she had started, she who never aged, and never changed. She had stopped, then. Stopped because the risk was too great and the visions too terrible. But they were trapped, and she was trapped by a tenuous promise.

Or freed from Apollo's curse— that she could have her dream of seeing the future but in denying him she brought upon herself the curse that no one would listen.

She flashed for an instant, remembering the serpents in the temple, soft motion across her body and tongues striking as they whispered their occult knowledge into her. She woke with the knowledge, woke with the vision, but she woke with the god, pale and slim, blood from the sacrifices on his lips and his eyes full of lust she denied.

Three serpents. Three women, linked.

"Who are you?"

But they were gone and the booth broken down and time had fled. The twins walked her back to her trailer and for the next 10 days the pattern repeated, the women coming after the show, the twins coming to escort her back. Mia for a week looking almost rosy, bright and full and awake, no longer sickly thin, just before she began to wane, and Lin, every night– "Let me in. Let me stay. You can have what you've always wanted– they will listen." And every night she refused him and slept alone and woke to find the ringmaster there, somehow afraid she was on the verge of escape.

Cassie, afraid of very much the same thing.

Until the tenth night.

"We can set you free," the women said.

"We can change all this," the first said alone. "As you changed everything before."

Sisters? Fates? Cassie was so exhausted she barely raised her head. Nine nights of them, unrelenting, promising promises that could not come to pass. Nine nights of dreams and nightmares, nine nights of pain when she spoke Truth and no one listened.

"Please," Cassie whispered, and they were gone. Illusions. Visions. They'd be there after the performances in the big top, and she needed no spark to know that. "Please."

"Help you set up?" Lin, and Mia. Bright and dark, Mia a thin and fading crescent, wrapped round herself, fading to her brother's glory.

Cassie managed a smile. "Thanks." She took Lin's hand and the night darkened and the sky exploded, pain tore through her mind and she saw it all at once, the night's show, jugglers and acrobats and high wire performers and bears, that poor sad damned bear the ringmaster had somehow caught– everyone in his circus was caught somehow– and she saw the wires falling and nets tearing, saw performers dropping and jugglers cut by their knives. She saw Lin and Mia, struggling together against the audience, desperate to escape the show as accidents and mistakes and mis-cues and the like turned deadly.

She saw fire.

No.

"Lin, listen to me," she said and took his arm between the blood, already bloody, had the show started? There were cuts across his chest, bright skin but Lin himself fading away from her. Her sight wavered with the force of the vision. From the other side of the big top she saw a flash and arc and knew it had already started. Fire. The tent would catch in an instant. Sawdust and straw. The entire big top was combustible.

Vision wavered. She stood outside the tent.

"Cassie? You up to this tonight?"

She reached for the hand Lin extended and stumbled against him. The show hadn't started. "Fire," she said and started forward. The three women stood in front of her and the pain came in a wave and drove her to her knees– the vision of a woman's face, and shattering glass, an accident she thought but this time she saw her own face.

She went to everyone. Roustabouts. Roadies. Temporary help, hired town to town and uniformly looking like people she'd avoid in a dark alley even without a spark. She went to performers and at last she went to the ringmaster.

"We can't go on tonight. There's going to be more accidents. There's going to be–" She hesitated, remembering the first time, her family in the stands. She'd only gone a couple minutes, looking for a place to relieve herself, and the spark had come too little, too late and no one had listened. At last she plunged into the ring between a line of elephants, and the ringmaster caught her before she could shout her warnings, caught her and snared her and she saw the spark that caught sawdust and canvas and begged, unabashed, until he relented.

She sealed her fate in the bargain.

He was watching her. The set of his mouth said he already knew what she hadn't said.

"Fire," Cassie said. "There's going to be a fire." She stopped, then, and said nothing more. Because he'd either hear her or he wouldn't. If he didn't, no amount of shouting would change it. Cassie ran her hands over her neck. She could still feel the serpent touch, the gliding along her throat and ears. She watched the ringmaster.

"If it's nothing important, Cassie, I suggest we have a performance to get ready for."

She couldn't tell with him. The ringmaster was made up of lies, a being surely old as Cassie herself. She couldn't tell if he'd heard her or not, only that he had turned away, already calling the performers to him, beginning the impromptu list, the schedule for this evening, who followed who.

Her energy left her in a rush. She sagged against tent supports. Her chest hurt. No tears. She'd never cried. Lost so many families over the years; it was why she chose to be alone now. Death always came in some form, except for her. Death came for everyone except those outside the natural order. Those set apart. Those touched by gods.

When she turned, the twins stood directly behind her, and for the first time they were uncloaked– unmasked and unhidden. The sun god held out his hand. His sister echoed the movement and Cassie let herself be pulled into their arms.

Vision fled; her other senses filled. There were mouths and hands and blood and the moon and the sun. Apollo stroked and murmured. His skin was hot under her hands and Cassie's tongue traced the blood on his chest, her hands moved across his biceps, hot flesh, skin like the sun and behind her Diana ran cold white hands across Cassie's shoulders, down her sides, curled round across her breasts, down to the tops of her thighs. It beat against her, the fire, the vision, the knowledge of what the night would bring. Her thoughts rippled and twisted, the three women tangled in her mind– three sisters, fates or oracles, sent or called to wake her, and the fire–

"The fire–"

"Hush," Apollo said. "They will listen."

They held her with tongues and fingers, with kisses and caresses. When the recorded fanfare began she jerked away from them, pale twins half-clothed, bloodied before the show even began. She ran, knowing her skirts were torn, her blouse askew and falling from her shoulders. She ran, barefoot, past the barkers and the temps, the handlers and the roadies, and found the ringmaster moments from his cue. The spotlight burned, waiting for him to step into it. Cassie grabbed his arm.

"Please."

For a moment her voice almost didn't come at all. She tasted the sun god's blood on her tongue and wondered if he'd left her mute, another punishment for some other crime.

The ringmaster blinked, and turned to her. Cassie saw herself reflected in his eyes, steel eyes. It was his big top. It was his show.

"Please," Cassie said softly. "Hear me. There's going to be a fire. Many people will die."

He looked at her without speaking for long seconds while the fire bloomed and grew in Cassie's mind, driven by the fear he meant to let the fire come, and then he turned from her all at once, as if heading simply to start the show. Over his shoulder he said, "Wait for me in your trailer," and then, just before he stepped into view of the crowds, "You smell like blood."

Cassie looked down. Her palms were criss-crossed with blood, cut from Lin's weapons. She took her first full breath in hours. Blood sacrifice.

Cassie moved to the curtained entrance to the big top and stood just at the edge, watching. Across the tent, up in the stands, just above the top bleacher, a light shorted. A cable short circuited. A blue line of energy streaked and caught canvas and the fire started. The big top wasn't filled. The top corner was empty. No one saw it.

"Please," Cassie whispered.

"Ladies and gentlemen, boys and girls, grandmothers and grandfathers and everyone else joining us tonight, welcome–" The ringmaster bowed to applause and straightened, top hat once more upon his head, showman to the finish. "Ladies and gentlemen, the show much go on. But just for this minute I must ask you to go on– if you would– slowly, calmly, if you would indulge us, we need you to exit the big top."

For the second time her energy left her in a rush. Cassie heard the ringmaster's voice continue, exhorting and cajoling and ordering the crowd from their seats. She heard him say one of the animals had gotten loose. She heard him say the tent wasn't quite secure. She heard him say one of the performers had come down with something contagious. Different stories meant for different ears. Whatever worked. There's a sucker born every minute– whatever It was, he told a handful that They were giving It away for free outside the tent.

Cassie pulled herself away from the support and leaned forward. Past the canvas curtains she saw the crowd and went still. Long dresses. Bustles. Hats she remembered as frighteningly heavy and uncomfortable. Men in suits, carrying gloves, and children in sailor suits and ringlets, sticky candy mouths and that never changed, but otherwise– and then, from across the tent, for just an instant she saw them. Husband, and child. Orderly and grim. Daniel had hold of Emily's hand, leading her, and she could see him looking for her, could feel the way his heart pounded, trying not to spook their daughter but terrified nonetheless. Before she thought about it she raised her arm and waved. Daniel waved back and motioned. He'd meet her outside the tent. Get *out*, go *around*. And then he was gone, Daniel and Emily out of sight, swallowed by the crowd and by time itself. The fire bloomed, sudden explosion as a gas light blew and caught another part of the tent on fire. Cassie saw the last of the crowd exit, blue jeans and sweat shirts, designer wear and super thrift. She stood for just a moment longer, then backed away from the tent. Blinding pain in her temples. She sparked, turned and ran, and behind her the tent went up in flames.

The fire spread. Even with all the safeguards and sprinklers, the big top went up and the sideshow caught and she heard the wailing of fire trucks coming but she didn't need to read the future to know they'd be too late to save much. Pain drove Cassie to her knees and she vomited blood into sawdust. When she stood she turned toward her trailer in time to watch as the fire hit the kerosene tanks and for just an instant she saw her face reflected in the window before the glass shattered and the trailer blew into the night sky. Cassie stood with her arms around herself, bloody palms smearing the fingerprints of the twins. When the blaze settled she saw all that was left of the trailer was broken axles and bent wheels. Cassie turned and walked away. The ringmaster had said to go back to her trailer. No one usually argued with the ringmaster. Therefore, he would think she was dead. And therefore–

"You are free," the women said. The blocked her path. Fates. Oracles. Muses. She no longer cared what they were. "Come with us," they said and held out their hands.

Cassie shook her head. "They'll listen now," she said. "I can help." She spread her hands and wondered if they'd understand and watched as the women twisted and coiled, slid back into their true shapes.

"We will wait," one said.

"We are eternal," said another.

"It is your gift," the third said.

Cassie turned and walked back the way she'd come.

When she reached her booth she saw the fire hadn't spread that far. All around her the circus was in uproar. Red and blue lights bathed the fire. Flames covered everything in autumnal glow. She moved along the edges, not wanting to attract attention. Her booth had not burned, but something or someone had knocked it down and it lay cracked and trampled. Her starred and scarred crystal ball lay nearby; the star cloth still wrapped part of it. Cassie ignored it, bent down instead to scoop up the plywood sign, a cheesy thing, cracked and splintered and warped. Across the background of bright blue, silver stars cavorted. Across the center it read: "What do the stars hold for YOU? Ask *our* star. Ask Cassandra."

She took the sign with her when she walked away.

Jennifer Rachel Baumer lives, writes, runs and procrastinates in the Northern Nevada desert where she lives with her husband and cats in the rural North Valleys, surrounded by jackrabbits, cottontails, coyotes and quail… and possibly ghosts.

www.ingramcontent.com/pod-product-compliance
Lightning Source LLC
Chambersburg PA
CBHW020626130626
46552CB00003B/1100